OUTLAW BREED

OUTLAW BREED

WILLIAM BYRON MOWERY

CUTTING EDGE

Originally Published as *The Black Automatic*

ISBN-13: 978-1-954840-10-2

Published by
Cutting Edge Books
PO Box 8212
Calabasas, CA 91372
www.cuttingedgebooks.com

CHAPTER ONE

THE telephone rang—startling in the quiet of the apartment. Wondering who was calling him so late at night, Noel put down his book and lifted the receiver.

A man's voice, a young and buoyant voice, came over the wire:

"Hullo! Inspector Irving?"

"This is Irving, yes," Noel answered. In dry tones he added, "But the 'Inspector' part of it is a trifle out of date, friend—I resigned from the Mounted four months ago."

"I know. I read all about that raw deal you got," the caller said. "That 'Inspector' was just a tongue-slip. Habit." He lowered his voice cautiously. "I say, Irving—I'd like to ankle around and have a powwow with you. Want to talk something over. Something important."

"Who's speaking?" Noel asked, frowning in perplexity. The voice was strange, and that "something important" seemed tinged with mystery.

"You never heard of me, so my name wouldn't mean anything," the man evaded. "And I can't discuss *this* business over a phone. I've got to see you personally, Irving, and right away. Please, partner."

Badly puzzled, Noel debated a moment. This midnight caller, who refused to disclose name or business, might be some old-time enemy, gunning for him. Equally possible, the man might really be a stranger. His urgent tones sounded as though he was in serious trouble and needed help.

"All right, come ahead," Noel bade, unwilling to refuse. "First apartment, left, ground floor."

He set the phone down, reached into a desk drawer for his black automatic, and slipped the weapon into his blouse pocket, not quite certain whether his visitor intended to greet him with a handclasp or a bullet. Wariness was long habit with him. His thirteen hectic years with the Mounted, and especially these last four years as head of the Secret Squad, had left him poor in dollars but unenviably rich in enemies and personal vengeances. There were men in prison, men of dangerous type, who swore to kill him when they walked free again. The narcotic runners of the West Coast hated him cordially, for good cause; and they were a sinister lot. And he felt reasonably sure that sometime, somewhere, some survivor of the demolished Rocco gang would try to rub him out, in retaliation for his killing Frank Rocco, last March.

Curious about this midnight visitor, he stepped over to the window, stood behind the heavy curtain to avoid making a target of himself, and watched the street in front of the building.

A long line of boulevard lights, half muffled by a ground fog and looking like a string of great translucent pearls, stretched down toward the heart of Winnipeg; but the city itself was asleep at that late hour, with only an occasional automobile or homing pedestrian still abroad. The night air was heavy with rose and snow flower from a little shrubbery plot outside; and the mid-July moon, circled with a rainbow corona, shone down through the mist, flooded in at the window and fell in a silvery pool on the cheap grass rug of the apartment.

The flower odors reminded Noel, poignantly, of his mother's rock garden in far-off Nova Scotia; and the thought occurred to him that instead of staying on in lonely Winnipeg, city of his disappointments and wrecked ambitions, perhaps he should go back to his boyhood home for a season or two. His people were dead, his former friends were long gone, but the sea and the quiet old fishing village still were there. In the healing peace of that seaside hamlet perhaps he could block out some sort of future for himself, now that his Mounted career had been unexpectedly dynamited.

And there, perhaps, he could become a human being once more, instead of a shadow and a hunter of men.

Discouraged and lonely, he gazed out across the sleeping city and wondered what new path he could possibly follow. Unless he took up private detective work, which he detested, he had no profession whatever. His experience, his brilliant record, his outstanding reputation in the Intelligence had suddenly become of no worth. He had spent thirteen years forging and tempering a good sword, and now the weapon was without use or value to him.

It was an infinitely disheartening task, this beginning all over again. With the best of his young manhood gone, with public opinion snapping at his heels like an ungrateful mongrel, he found himself, at thirty-three, on one of those dead centers of life where the past was buried beyond resurrection and the future was an utter blank.

But the wasted years and the rank injustice of the Rocco case did not weigh on him half so heavily as his isolation from the warm living world of men and women. As he stood there by the window, in the deep hush of midnight, he felt cruelly alone, without friend or relative on earth. For thirteen years he had led a shadowy and uprooted existence, burying his identity, working in lone-handed secrecy. Cut off from normal human relationships, he had been little more than a name and departmental number, following trails all over the Dominion and abroad.

In consequence now, as an ironic reward of his years to Force and society, he could look out across this city of a quarter-million and think of no one whom he could truly call friend....

Down the mist-dim boulevard a dark figure emerged from the fog, crossed the street at a diagonal and headed for the apartment building.

With his left hand in his blouse pocket, Noel moved away from the window and turned the desk lamp so that it shone on the door. Then he stepped over beside a dark portière and quietly waited.

He intended, if the visitor was an enemy, to get the drop and disarm the man and throw him out. That would be neater and more professional than a gun argument.

At the person's knock, a few moments later, he invited, "Come in."

The door opened, and a man stepped inside.

With a swift expert glance Noel sized his visitor up, as the latter stood there in the light. A stalwart young chap of twenty-three, dressed in cords and boots and leather jacket, the man was a complete stranger. His clothes and weather-darkened face and the rugged virility about him, all hinted strongly of the outdoors. His black eyes and the boyish wave in his thick black hair were as instantly likable as his cheerful voice had been on the phone.

Not seeing his host by the darkish drapery, the youngster stared around in puzzled fashion, blinking his eyes and frowning. At last he caught sight of Noel, and his face lighted up with a smile.

"Irving!" He strode across the room, hand outstretched. "Mighty glad to meet you! Hated to come busting in on you this late, but I *had* to." Probing, curious, his glance roamed over the gray-eyed silent man confronting him. "So you're Noel Irving! From all I've read about you and all the long-haired yarns a person hears about you, I imagined you as older—and harder." Then his glance met Noel's, and he saw the cold glinty quality in the eyes of the ex-officer, and his face sobered. "By the Lord," he said, "you might be plenty hard, at that!"

Noel invited courteously, "Sit down, please," and he motioned at the comfortable desk chair. Over their handshake he had noticed a suspicious bulge in his visitor's jacket pocket and knew that the bulge meant a hidden gun; but this young chap was plainly no criminal or enemy; and he took his own hand from his automatic.

With sharp, observant eyes he studied the young stranger, as the latter lit a cigarette. Whoever the man was and whatever had brought him here, he was emphatically no city person. Yet none of the ordinary outdoor types—prospector, timber cruiser, whatnot—seemed to fit him or seemed big enough to hold him. In the full flush of youth and self-confidence, he gave impression of being some foot-loose adventurer looking for worlds to conquer.

"Since you know my name," Noel remarked, sitting down on the couch, "I'm tempted to remind you of the quaint old custom known as introducing oneself."

The young stranger laughed. "Call me 'Jimmy,' " he said. "That much is correct, and it'll do as a handle for the present."

Noel eyed his visitor thoughtfully. "A cagey young devil," he decided. "Before telling me his name or business, he intends to sound me out. In the name of heaven *who is he?*"

Though he seldom made snap judgments, he instinctively liked this hard-bitten enigma who had come to him out of the moonlight and mist of a Winnipeg night. The youngster's buoyant cheerfulness was as invigorating as a breath of pine-spiked air. With his rare smile and warm good will he barged his way into a person's friendship like a young bull moose through a thicket of buckbrush.

Jimmy picked up the open book on the desk, glanced at it, whistled. "Latin! The *Georgics!* Jeerusalem, partner, d'you actually read that stuff for pleasure? I once got as far as '*Arma virumque cano,*' but there I said: 'To hell with it! Too many girls and airplanes and good times in the world to monkey around with ablative absolutes'——"

Noel interrupted him. Sixty seconds of reading Jimmy's actions and manner had given him a rough idea of his guest's trouble; and he was uneasy.

"Jimmy," he asked quietly, with no intention of displaying professional wizardry, "are you sure that those men didn't trail you here to my apartment?"

The unexpected question dumbfounded Jimmy. "Hell's b-bells!" he gasped. His cigarette dropped from his fingers, and he stared wide-eyed at Noel, as though at a clairvoyant. "How did *you* know anything—uh—I mean, uh——" He broke off, got hold of himself again and picked up his cigarette. "What men? What're you talking about?"

Noel smiled. "No use, Jimmy. You're carrying a piece of hardware in your pocket; when you crossed the boulevard out there, a few minutes ago, you *looked back* twice; when that car went past just now, you listened with both ears to make sure that it didn't slow up or stop; and——"

"Don't!" Jimmy burst out, dropping his useless denial. "Don't go on. *You* know! And quit looking at me like that. You make me feel like an insect on a pin. Lord, I didn't realize, myself, that I did those things, and here you see 'em and see what's behind 'em and tell me all about it!"

"That sort of observation has been my work for years. I ought to be fairly competent at it."

"Competent?" Jimmy snorted. "Artistic, fellow! Downright artistic. No wonder they brought you all the way back from Shanghai, when the Federal men and the rest of the Mounted couldn't bag Frank Rocco. And no wonder it didn't take you long to have him hanging out on the line to dry!"

"Better answer my question about those men, Jimmy—are you in danger?"

"Not tonight."

"Then why are you all on edge?"

"Just jittery. Been playing tag with those mothers' sons long enough to jitter anybody's nerve. But I shook 'em, a while ago. Down town. They'll cold-trail me, all righto, and I'd better be scarce tomorrow; but tonight——" He leaned back comfortably and blew a lazy smoke ring ceilingward. "Say, it feels funny—and mighty good, Irving!—to breathe a safe breath for once."

Noel merely nodded. Quite evidently these "mothers' sons" were trying to kill Jimmy. They must have been hounding him for days or even weeks, playing this grim tag game in which "it" meant death for the lone-handed youngster.

"A city gang, Jimmy?" he asked, rather certain that they were not.

Jimmy laughed scornfully. "I wish they were! I could handle a fieldful of alley rats. But this outfit, they're *men*. They're brainy and tough, and they hang onto a fellow's trail like a pack of March wolves."

"An outfit, you say? How many men?"

"I don't know. Half a dozen anyhow. Likely more. I can't say exactly. They're so—so—damned ghostlike. You can't see 'em, can't fight 'em; you just know they're there and they've got you on the spot."

"Ghostlike? Isn't that a bit imaginative?"

Somewhat indignantly Jimmy pulled open his jacket and shirt and disclosed a long ugly knife-scar, just above his heart. "D'you call that imagination? I got that for failing to barricade my cabin door one night."

"Hmmph! I stand corrected."

Jimmy buttoned his shirt, tapped the ashes from his cigarette and looked again at Noel. "It's none of my business, Irving, but are you planning to go back with the Mounted? I've been thinking you might, as soon as this Rocco dust has settled a bit."

It was an outright honest question, and Noel answered it frankly. "No. As one newspaper put it, my usefulness in the Mounted is ended. And I wouldn't go back if I could. I'm done."

"Don't blame you," Jimmy grunted. "If I'd given thirteen years to the public and then the public turned around and gave me a kick in the pants, I'd have a bellyful too. The idiots!—making a Robin Hood out of a bloody-handed killer like Rocco." An anger blew across Jimmy's face, and he clenched his big fists as though wanting to go out and give the general public a licking.

"The fault was partly mine," Noel stated, grateful to this friendly young stranger who was championing him so sincerely. "I should have taken Rocco alive, Jimmy. In an open trial the Federals and we Mounted could have stripped all the glory clothes from Rocco and showed him up as just a sordid dollar-snatcher. But when I dynamited him in that cabin I made a hero of him—and a coward of myself."

He leaned forward, opened a desk drawer and tossed Jimmy a newspaper clipping. "Read that. It's typical of the stories on the morning of the break."

Jimmy turned the clipping to the light and scanned it aloud.

Rocco is dead. The spectacular desperado who flashed like a meteor across the world of crime is dead today. At 9 o'clock last night at a little lake between Winnipeg and the Border the notorious criminal and gang leader who defied the Police of two nations and had more than a dozen gangs shot out from under him but always escaped himself was trapped in a lonely cabin rendezvous, along with three of his lieutenants and two women of the underworld, by Inspector Noel Irving and a Mounted detail; and his career replete with hairbreadth escapes ended in death. Not in a gallant death, shooting it out with his enemies, as Frank Rocco would have chosen, but in sudden and violent oblivion—blown to eternity by a bomb barrage, without being given a chance to cut his way out with blazing guns....

With a gesture of contempt Jimmy threw the clipping aside and brushed his fingers. "I see. When you dynamited him, you gave the romancers their chance. Didn't you realize you were blowing him to glory?"

"I had little choice. That cabin hangout was a regular arsenal, and those fellows were armed with everything from bombs to machine guns. We had nothing but pocket automatics. If I had risked a fight, Rocco would probably have got away, and several of my men would have been killed. Rather than sacrifice them, I crept up to that cabin myself and tossed five dynamite sticks through the window."

"Those two women in there—that's what really started the avalanche against you. wasn't it?"

"Yes. That rubbed the public the wrong way. I didn't know of any women in that cabin. Sergeant Spencer and I had watched that hangout all afternoon, through binoculars, and we saw no sign of those two. But nobody believed us."

Jimmy toyed absently with the pull-cord of the lamp. "Anyhow, you took Rocco, after everybody else had failed. That ought to be some satisfaction."

Noel winced. Bitter the satisfaction he had found in Frank Rocco's death. He had killed the man but not the myth. The secret glorification of Rocco as a gallant and heroic figure, was still alive, working an immense amount of social harm. The man was passing into legend; and all that the Mounted and the Federals could ever say about Frank Rocco could never explode that pernicious myth now.

In his abrupt way Jimmy plunged into the reason of his visit. "Well, now that I'm sure about you and the Mounted, I can lay down my cards. Irving, some time ago I stumbled onto a pot of luck. It's a big proposition. A life-time chance. I thought I could swing the job by myself. But then this pack of slinkers got after me; and they've got me out on a bad limb.

"In a nutshell, I need help and a partner. Highpower help and a partner I can bank on to the limit. You'd be both. With a little help from me *you* can splash these men. I picked you out of a whole Dominion-full of people as the only man who can smack 'em down. After that we'd have clear sailing; we'd clean up handsome; and we'd have a rattling good time a-doing it."

Partly because of his loneliness, partly because of the challenge in this unknown venture, that word "partner" struck a secret response in Noel. In a general way he could imagine nothing finer than to shake the bitter dust of Winnipeg from his feet, team up with this leather-faced Jimmy, and pitch off with him on the adventure trail, wherever that trail might lead.

"Now get this," Jimmy went on, tapping the desk to emphasize his words. "This proposition of mine is no wild-goose chase or wishful thinking. It's a hard fact. A reality. I've got it right in my hand. Man, I've *got* it! If we can only tie a knot in this outfit's tail, we'll both be wealthy men inside a year."

Through the smoke of his cigarette Noel eyed Jimmy, trying to make him out. Who was this extraordinary youngster? Where did he come from and what was this tight-guarded secret of his? And these men hounding him, half a dozen against one—who were they?

"Jimmy," he asked, "why didn't you go to the regular Mounted for help, instead of to me, a stranger and a civilian?"

"I told you why. You can handle these fellows. The mine-run Mounted couldn't."

"That's not your only reason. Jimmy, you didn't *dare* go to the Mounted. You're hiding your identity. You wouldn't tell me your name; I can see where you tore the dealer label from your jacket; and there above your left wrist you've even burned off a tattoo mark. Now, Jimmy, you're keeping yourself anonymous because this job of yours is illegal. You're doing something outside the law. Right?"

Jimmy fidgeted uneasily. "Well, uh, I guess ... Yes, it *is* illegal. We could be sent to the pen. That's honest. But there's not a chance in a hundred that we'll get caught. That's honest too. And there's nothing wrong about this job, Irving. It's illegal but not wrong."

"What do you consider 'wrong,' Jimmy?"

" 'Wrong' is when you hurt somebody else."

"Hmmph. Not a bad definition. And you, in your conscience, don't consider this job wrong?"

"I don't! We wouldn't be harming a soul on earth——"

He broke off there, abruptly, frozen to silence by a gesture of warning from Noel. In the shrubbery plot outside, some stray dog had growled—a sinister throaty snarl; and to Noel's ears had come the slight scratchy noise of a rose-briar scraping against a man's trouser-leg. The little sound made his blood run cold. Jimmy's enemies *had* trailed the youngster. They were lurking outside in that shrubbery. They were lining aim on Jimmy, by the light of the desk lamp.

Without moving or in any way betraying his discovery, he glanced at the window, out of the corner of his eye. In the moon-shadow of a lilac bush a dark splotch, a man-figure, was slowly rising up; and from another bush came a moon-glint on gun steel.

"Jimmy"—he spoke in a sharp whisper—"they're outside, those men. Just outside the window. Don't turn, don't look. For heaven's sake do what I tell you, and quick! If you look, they'll shoot, they'll riddle you. Give that lamp cord a sudden yank, then lunge behind this couch. In the dark we can shoot it out with them."

Instead of obeying him, Jimmy jerked his head around and stared at the window. Evidently he saw one of those shadowy forms outside, for he leaped to his feet and defiantly whipped out his gun.

"Get down!" Noel cried at him. "Here—here, with me!" Unable to reach the lamp cord in time, he grabbed a footstool and arched it up, to crash it against the light and plunge the room into darkness.

He was a split-second too late. As his arm went back, as Jimmy stood fumbling with the trigger safety of his gun, a spurt of fire leaped from the lilac bush; a pane of glass shattered and fell in bits to the rug; the *kr-oo-mm* of a heavy automatic bellowed in at the window.

From the dark shrubbery a second gun opened up. Through screen, glass and curtain the two automatics poured a hail of bullets at the defiant youngster by the desk. The window curtain twitched crazily. The room was filled with the vicious *th-uu-pp* and *splaat* of bullets smashing into the desk and chair and wall beyond.

Oblivious of danger to himself, Noel sprang from behind the shelter of the couch, jerked out his automatic and began shooting at those livid flashes, to silence them and save Jimmy.

He heard a yelp, the cry of a man hard-hit by one of his bullets; but those two guns kept up their murderous blast, As a heavy slug struck the lamp and shattered it, Noel had one anguished glimpse of Jimmy clutching at his breast, collapsing into the chair and then toppling to the floor.

Abruptly the blast from the shrubbery stopped. On the heels of the last shot a laugh flounced in through the shattered window—a mocking brutal laugh at the spectacle of Jimmy crumpling and falling.

In the dead quiet, broken only by Jimmy's hoarse breathing as he lay there on the rug, Noel heard the swish of bushes, the quick *pad-pad* of running feet; and it came home to him that those men, after their swoop and deadly strike at Jimmy, were making their get-away.

The thought of their escaping touched off a fury in him. Dropping his own empty gun, he stooped down and tore the automatic from Jimmy's hand, sprang to the window, brushed aside the curtain, flung the window high, broke the screen loose, and vaulted outside upon the gravel.

The patter of running feet had silenced. He listened intently, heard nothing. He ran out to the sidewalk and glanced up and down the misty boulevard. Nothing. Not a glimpse or sound or vanishing blur.

Unable to believe that those men could have disappeared so quickly, he hurried back, gun in hand, to the lilacs and rose arbor, and kicked into the black shadows. But the men were gone, as phantomlike as they had come. Without a wasted motion or second, they had appeared, struck, vanished. One of them had been wounded badly; yet they had managed a clean get-away. That blur in the lilac shadow, the burst of fire, the dying patter of feet—that was all he had seen or heard.

He climbed back through the window, swearing savagely at himself for having taken Jimmy's assurance that those men had been shaken off. Throughout his talk with Jimmy he had been vaguely uneasy. Now he realized he should have obeyed his own judgment. He snapped on a light, gathered up his young guest and laid him on the couch.

Riddled by a half a dozen bullets, Jimmy was pallid and limp; he was breathing in weak gasps; his shirt, where he had clutched at himself, was sodden with blood.

For all his experiences with crime and death, Noel was badly shaken as he bent over Jimmy, and a mist came to his eyes. His strange young friend, so full of buoyant life only a few minutes ago, lying there stricken now, with all the surging vitality shot out of him—it seemed incredible and a little ghastly. He refused to believe that Jimmy could be dying; but the weak pulse, the waxen color of the youngster's face, made him afraid. Working swiftly, he slipped a cushion under Jimmy's head, loosened his clothes, brushed a straggle of hair from his forehead.

"Jimmy! Who were those men?" he demanded, realizing that he had to pull the youngster back to consciousness and pry a few words out of him or those words might never be spoken. "Where are they from? And you, Jimmy—who are *you?*"

Jimmy's eyes flickered open, and he stared up at Noel in the groping way of a person sinking into the dark of unconsciousness. He whispered, brokenly: "The damned—slinkers! They—tagged me—all right—partner——"

At the door of the apartment somebody was pounding and hammering. "Irving! Irving! What the devil happened in there?"

Noel recognized the voice as an apartment neighbor's, a city policeman who lived across the corridor. "Come in, Yates," he bade. And when the man entered, with flashlight and service revolver, Noel jerked a thumb at the phone. "Get Mounted Headquarters down town. Talk to Sergeant Herm Spencer. Tell Spencer that I want him here on the jump. Then call a hospital ambulance. Tell 'em to make it *fast*. Come alive, man!—don't stand there pop-eyed."

He turned again to the couch and tried desperately to rouse Jimmy. One word or name or tangible fact from the youngster's own lips would be priceless.

"Jimmy! What's your name, your *last* name? And those men—who are they?" He shook Jimmy's arm, roughly, for the precious seconds were fleeting. "Don't let go, partner. Talk to me!" Jimmy did not answer or stir.

Yates came over to the couch. "I got Spencer. He's on the way. The ambulance too." He gazed down at the unconscious Jimmy. "Who is this fellow, Irving?"

"I don't know."

Yates picked up Noel's warm gun from the floor, turned it over in his palm, cleared his throat. "It, uh, wasn't you that shot him, was it?"

"For Christ's sake, didn't you hear that bang-whanging outside the window? And that laugh, when they saw him fall? I was shooting at those men out there. Bring me some water—a cold towel for his face. He mustn't slip away without talking."

"It'll take more'n cold water to bring *him* back," the policeman remarked, turning toward the tiny kitchen. "He's a goner. That's your ambulance coming—from the hospital."

Noel raised his head, listened to the screechy siren. When he looked again at Jimmy, he suddenly started, bent closer, felt for a pulse beat, found none . . . .

Yates came back with the towel. "Here." But Noel shook his head, silently, without glancing up.

For a few moments longer he knelt there by the couch, his fingers tightening upon the limp hand of the brave young stranger who had come to him for help and had found death instead. "Jimmy," he muttered, once or twice. And: "They laughed. They killed you and *laughed*."

As the siren drew near and stopped in front of the apartment building, he stood up, slowly, and turned to Yates.

"Please go out to them," he said. "Tell them that they're not needed here—now."

CHAPTER TWO

AT THE coroner's inquest, the next morning, Noel found himself under suspicion and at bay. In the little courtroom, tense and hushed, he could feel this suspicion beating against him like a hostile wave.

Of the thirty-odd people present—coroner, witnesses, jury, reporters, Superintendent Ostrand of the Mounted, and the curiosity-mongers crowded around the walls—no one believed, indeed, that this unknown Jimmy had been killed by the hand of Noel Irving. But upon them all rested the conviction that the ex-Inspector had known Jimmy and the actual killers and was more or less guiltily implicated in the murder of last night.

In the entire room Noel's one defender was the man sitting beside him, Sergeant Herm Spencer, his former subordinate and long-time associate on the Secret Squad.

To the inquest and the hostile suspicion Noel paid little attention. As he sat there, cold and aloof, a battle was raging within him, a battle which not even Spencer knew anything about.

With unseeing eyes he gazed at the exhibit table where lay Jimmy's gun and shirt, some empty cartridges from the shrubbery plot, some battered slugs picked out of the apartment walls, and a few other odds and ends of "evidence." In so far as he paid any attention at all to the proceedings, Noel smiled disdainfully at this worthless display, at the coroner's fussy importance, at Superintendent Ostrand's air of vast professional wisdom, at the hopeless inadequacy of this little court and these clumsy amateurs to make headway against the dark mystery of Jimmy's death.

For hours last night he himself, with Spencer's expert help, had worked on the crime; had worked with infinite patience and in grim earnest; but of Jimmy's identity and secret and of clue to those uncanny shadows, he discovered nothing.

At the coroner's request Sergeant Spencer stood up to testify. He was brief and trenchant.

"I got there ten minutes after the shooting. Mr. Irving and I worked till morning on the case. For some reason this young fellow, Jimmy, had wanted to hide his identity. He certainly had done a complete job of it. Besides cutting all the dealer labels from his clothes and burning a tattoo mark from his arm, he'd removed all papers from his pockets and billfold and had filed the serial number off his gun.

"We don't know who he was, where he appeared from or what this 'pot of luck' was that he mentioned, or who those men are or why they hounded and killed him. I can't add one item to the account which Mr. Irving has already given you."

As the coroner's physician rose to testify and drew the attention of the room, Spencer slipped a little picture from his pocket and cupped it in his palm so that only he and Noel could see it. A tiny faded snapshot, cut to the size and shape of a silver dollar, the picture was the one bit of evidence which they had kept to themselves, for humane reasons.

"Take another look at this, Noel," Spencer whispered. "She might be among this crowd."

"She's not. I've already looked."

"I must say," Spencer commented, "that Jimmy picked a winner for his girl friend. She's downright lovely, Noel."

"His girl friend? Don't jump to conclusions. For all we know, she might be his sister. She resembles him a lot."

"Sister? Did you ever see a fellow carry his sister's picture in his watch-case? Neither did I! I'm going to keep an eye on the morgue and on Jimmy's funeral. She might show up."

Noel glanced down again at the tiny photograph; at the black-haired beautiful girl looking up at him from the palm of Spencer's hand. She did resemble Jimmy, remarkably. Her hair and eyes were black, like his; her nose and high intelligent forehead seemed feminine counterparts of Jimmy's; the fine glowing vitality about her was like a softened echo of Jimmy's splendid buoyancy.

Spencer proffered him the photograph. "You seem interested. I won't need it any more."

Noel took the picture, crumpled it, tore it to tiny bits; and as Spencer stared at him, astonished he said:

"That picture was dangerous, Herm. To that girl. It might have got away from us and into the papers. It won't now. The tabloids won't make any Roman holiday out of that girl now. Whoever she is or whatever her relationship was to Jimmy, I believe she's of decent sort. If you do contact this girl, shield her. Don't let her get dragged through the notoriety of a murder case."

When the last witness had testified, Superintendent Ostrand rose impressively to his feet.

"Mr. Coroner, with your permission *I* would like to question the, ah, principal witness."

"Certainly, sir. Go right ahead."

Across the table Noel met the gaze of his former Officer Commanding. As a Division head and a man of prestige, Ostrand could have saved him from the Rocco backfire; but the officer had not lifted a hand to still the public clamor. Though a competent enough administrator, with long years of service at Ottawa, Ostrand had risen to his high rank chiefly because he was a calculating climber who knew how to pull the right wires, choose the right associates, go to the right church and right social functions, marry right, and always gauge public opinion right. He blew with the main wind; and he was doing that now, in this little courtroom, across the gun and blood-stained shirt of the dead Jimmy.

"Irving," he said sternly, "after listening carefully to your account and the other evidence, it is *my* opinion that you are deliberately withholding information vital to this case."

A ripple of applause passed around the room. Noel sat cold and silent. With a gracious nod to his audience for their approval, Ostrand went on:

"Your story about this midnight phone call, midnight visitor and midnight killers is too flimsy for a man of *my* experience to believe." Dramatically he pointed an accusing finger. "Noel Irving, you are concealing something about this murder!"

The applause broke out again. Herm Spencer went red-faced with anger at the spectacle of the smug wealthy Ostrand baiting the penniless and disgraced ex-officer; but Noel himself did not move or change expression.

Exasperated by his silence, Ostrand fired a final threat at him:

"Very well! Since you choose to be recalcitrant, let me warn you that I intend to push this case and arrest those men; and if I discover that you did obstruct justice here, then you're going to suffer the full penalty of the law."

Noel smiled in derision at Ostrand's vow to take that shadowy outfit. On this case Ostrand and the city police and the regular Mounted were hopelessly beyond their depth. That outfit was no city gang, fitting into some ordinary pigeonhole, but a pack of outlanders, strange and unguessable. Whoever picked up their trail would be good, and whoever ran that trail would likely wind up dead, like Jimmy.

The jury filed out, to deliberate their verdict privately. The tense quiet of the room broke, the hum of low voices arose; and Noel went back to that battle within himself.

In vision he saw Jimmy coming across the room to him last evening; felt his strong handclasp and the warmth of his smile;

heard the young adventurer calling him "partner." Jimmy had been his guest, killed in his home; and by a law as ancient as the human home itself it was his solemn duty to see that Jimmy was avenged.

He reflected, too, that somewhere in the Dominion there was a pack of men brazen enough, confident enough, disdainful enough of the Mounted, that they had slain a man in the very abode of one who had led the Mounted Intelligence for years. They had flung a challenge at the might and the majesty of the Law. That challenge must not go unanswered. Somebody *had* to take up that gage.

In a few minutes the jury shuffled back in with their verdict, and the foreman read it. Of those tedious Whereas's and Aforesaid's, only six words lingered with Noel—"at the hands of parties unknown." How true those words, he thought. And forever those parties would remain unknown. Like wraiths those men had faded into the mist last night, with a wanton laugh. Today, somewhere, they were alive, in the sunshine; and Jimmy, in that gray old building down the street——

The inquest broke up. Spencer turned to Noel. "You're lucky that they didn't vote some crazy charge against you. Let's get out of here."

Noel scarcely heard him. In the moments just past he had lost the battle which had been raging within him since last midnight. In bitterness of heart he had sworn that he would never again lay hand to Police work or go back into that shadow world where he had wasted thirteen years of his life. But now he had to go back. Inexorably he was driven by conscience and duty and personal vengeance to go after those unknowns. The good sword which he had spent thirteen years in forging and polishing and which he had vowed never to use again—well, he must use it once more, for Jimmy's sake.

Spencer took him by the arm. "Come home with me, Noel. You need a rest. You're done out."

Noel shook his head, slowly. "Thanks, Herm. Before I rest there's a little matter to be attended to."

With a nod of "so long" he turned abruptly and shouldered his way up the crowded aisle for the door.

Three nights later, carrying a dufflebag that contained a few clothes and personal belongings, Noel called around at Sergeant Spencer's home, near one o'clock.

He found Spencer hard at work at a table in the little living room. Tired and harassed, the sergeant was combing through a mass of fingerprint keys, rogue-gallery snaps and various paraphernalia from the Mounted files. On a couch across the room Eleanor Spencer was lying asleep, a blanket over her, a magazine and a half-eaten apple on the blanket.

"Where the devil have you been these last three days?" Spencer greeted him. "I drove around to your place a dozen times, and rang your phone bell off."

"I've been busy, Herm. If you've got a cup of coffee to spare, let's go back to the kitchen, where we can talk."

He stepped across to the couch, snapped off the reading light that was shining in Eleanor's face, and followed the sergeant back to the little white-tiled kitchen.

It was seldom he visited the Spencer home. The pleasantness of it, the very evident affection between those two, always gave him a bad twinge, in comparison with his own isolated existence.

"I found your note under my door," he said, as Spencer poured two cups of coffee. "So Ostrand is riding you, is he?"

"Worse than that. He's greasing the bamboo slide for me, Noel. Wants one of his Ottawa men in my place. My days with the Police are numbered. Look, he saddled me with this Jimmy case and told me to get results 'or else' ... It looks like 'or else' for me. I've worked day and night, I've got nowhere, and the trail's cold now. If you don't help me get started, I'm sunk."

Noel stirred the sugar in his coffee. "I'm glad you are stalled. You've got no business on this case. It's dangerous. It's tender dynamite. You've no right to take chances." He motioned at the living room, where Eleanor lay asleep. "You're married, Herm. Before snow flies you'll be a daddy. Get off this case and stay off."

"How can I? If I put up a kick, Ostrand'll bust me down to a buck cop."

"Let me tell you what to do. Go to Ostrand tomorrow and inform him that you've struck a hot scent. Ask him for six or seven weeks on the loose, with plenty of expense money. Then slip off somewhere, with Eleanor, and have a real vacation. You rate one. You haven't cashed a furlough in three years."

Spencer scowled. "You needn't joke. This is no joking matter."

"I mean exactly what I said. If you stick on duty here you'll have to produce some result; but if you're gone——"

"But I'd have to come back sometime, wouldn't I—and what would I have to show for my time?"

"You may have plenty. I hope to nail this outfit in the meanwhile; and if I do I'll see that you get part credit for the job."

Spencer's eyes popped open. "Are *you* going to start on this?"

"I've started! In the last three days I've dug up a lead, such as it is. I'm leaving Winnipeg tonight. I came round here to ask if you'd give me a little ride in your car. Just north of town. I'd taxi except that it's healthier to slip away on the quiet."

"Why, I'll—sure I'll take you; but—d'you really mean that you've pried the lid off this case already?"

"Miles from that. I've merely uncovered a promising lead. I'll tell you about it on our drive. Swallow your coffee and let's be traveling." …

Along the shore of a little resort lake a few miles north of the city, Spencer stopped the car and switched off the lights.

"Keep your gun handy," Noel warned, as they stepped out. "I believe those slinkers left Winnipeg four nights ago; but if they didn't, they're on the lookout here."

Silent and alert, they crept down through a drogue of poplars to the lake edge, where a small pier jutted out into deep water.

Though it was not yet three o'clock, the stars were beginning to dim, and the first gray of dawn was reaching up into the eastern sky. A light morning wind was rippling the lake and *laplapping* the wavelets against the boats at anchor in the shallows.

"How'd you find out that Jimmy was a flyer?" Spencer asked, glancing around for lurking shadows.

"His boots. The wear on his boots."

"I saw that wear myself. Thought it was auto pedals."

"No, no. With an auto there's extra wear on the right foot. With the rudder bars of a plane the wear is the same on both feet."

They started out upon the pier. At the far end of it a dark object, larger than the boats, slowly took on outline and resolved itself into a small monoplane, securely anchored and moored.

Noel pointed. "Jimmy came to Winnipeg in that plane, Herm. It has his fingerprints all over it."

"How'd you ever locate it, out here?"

"Hard work. I visited all the air fields and landing lakes within striking distance of town."

"What a little beauty!" Spencer remarked, eying the craft. A trim swift Diomede, with tiny three-place cabin, ruddered pontoons, and canvas hood drawn over its radial, it was rocking on the wavelets like a creature asleep. "With a plane like that a fellow could go strange places and do tall things. What luck did you have tracing its registry?"

"Mighty little. It was bought new in Seattle eighteen months ago. It dropped out of sight then and it's never been heard of since. It's what the Air Bureau calls a 'ghost plane'—unregistered, unlicensed, its whereabouts unknown. If Jimmy carried any license or papers, they were faked. He kept this plane as anonymous as he kept himself."

With Spencer following, he stepped down upon a pontoon, unlocked the little cabin, climbed in and snapped on his pocket flash. Leaning across toward the left rear window, he pressed on a silver-colored button which looked, at first glance, like an ordinary upholstering brad. A panel beneath the window dropped down and exposed a small compartment roughly the size of a brief-case.

From the little niche Noel drew out a pair of silver-fox pelts. Beautiful Keewatin furs, perfectly matched, with long king-hairs and soft rich pelage, the pelts were so exquisite and lovely that Spencer unthinkingly reached out and stroked them.

"Jimmy bought these two silvers," Noel stated, "for that girl in his watch, but he had no chance to give them to her before he was killed. But what I wanted to show you is this." He rolled back one of the pelts to the "raw" side and pointed to a red-and-blue stenciling. "These are stamped furs. Royalty stamp. Those serial numbers gave me my lead on Jimmy. He bought these furs six days ago, at McMurray."

"Fort McMurray? That little jumping-off place over northwest in the Athabasca?"

"Yes. He was there at McMurray last Thursday. That's all on earth I know about him, and I don't know anything about these outlanders. I'm flying over there in hopes I can pick up his trail and back-track him. Wherever he came from, there I'll find these men."

"You're using *this* plane?"

"Yes."

"Heavens! Why, it's a dead give-away. Those men know this ship. They'll know you're after 'em. They'll hop you."

"That's what I want. That's how it's got to be. I don't know who they are. I'm using this plane deliberately, to lure them into some overt act."

"It'll be overt, all right," Spencer agreed. "You'll lure 'em, all right. Man, you're using yourself as live bait!"

"I've got no other way of contacting them."

As they stepped back upon the pier, Spencer burst out: "Look here—I'm going along on this job! If you go alone you'll get killed. Those men'll know that you're Irving. They won't let you live twenty-four hours. Two guns are better than one, Noel. You and I've stood leg-to-leg on several tough jobs——"

Noel cut him short. "You're not going to make a widow out of Eleanor. I can gamble but you can't." With a glance at the eastern sky, where the gray light was broadening, he bade: "Help me get this plane ready to hit the air. I want to be two hundred miles from Winnipeg when day breaks."

They stripped the canvas from the radial, pulled up the toy anchor, untied the mooring ropes and swung the Diomede lakeward.

Silent, downcast, Spencer stood on a pontoon to say goodbye; and Noel, reading his gloomy fears, said to him:

"Stop worrying about me, Herm. I'll take care of myself. I always have." The words sounded hollow to his own ears. For him the trail ahead, against unknown enemies and into unknown dangers, was like a leap into a dark chasm. But he kept his voice cheerful and reached out his hand. "Well, here's shoving off, old man. If I win this trick—and I feel I'm going to—I'll bring these men back and turn 'em over to you. If I lose, I'll send you a wireless from hell and tell you who they are."

CHAPTER THREE

OVER the nose of his plane Noel looked north, across a range of timbered hills, and saw the Forks of the Clearwater and Athabasca, and spotted Fort McMurray, nestling between the two big rivers.

From his height of eleven thousand feet the little steel-end hamlet, glinting in the afternoon sun, seemed hardly the size of a postage stamp. Its single street was a mere ant run, and its buildings were microscopic dots of brown and white.

Flexing the stiffness from his arms and legs, he made ready for the ticklish job of a pontoon landing. The lengthy hours of flight that day across the prairie provinces had tired him, rusty as he was at piloting; and the long "dry hop" from Edmonton north to McMurray, over waterless country where a konking engine would have meant a fatal crack-up for his pontooned Diomede, had driven him high up into the fleecy woolpack and kept him on nervous edge for the last two hundred miles.

As he looked down at the river hamlet, a tingle of uneasiness ran through him. Without a doubt Jimmy's enemies, or at least some sharp-eyed scouts for them, were yonder at that little town. Regardless of whether McMurray had been Jimmy's base or merely a port of call, it was a strategic post, the jumping-off place for the entire North; and those men would not leave it unguarded.

Herm Spencer's warning, "Man, you're using yourself as live bait!" jigged unpleasantly across his thoughts. When he stepped ashore at McMurray he would be a marked man, marked for death. And he would not know who his enemies were till they had struck at him. It was like trying to locate a rattlesnake by groping around in its covert till it lashed at you—and trusting to luck that you could dodge its strike.

From the Forks his eyes followed the winding Athabasca on into the north, across a hundred miles of savage muskeg wilderness; and he had his first glimpse of the real Northland. An awe crept over him as he gazed to the dim watery horizon. The strangeness and huge immensity of that Three Rivers region fairly staggered him.

"And that," he breathed, "all that country yonder—that's only the *beginning* of the North!" In his mind's eye he saw those wild lands stretching on and on down north, past the Great Barrens and sub-Arctic Rockies, to the Polar Ocean two thousand miles away.

Truly this vast unpeopled country, basking under the midnight sun in summer and ravaged by sixty-below storms through its long white winter, had been a fit stamping ground for the hard-bitten Jimmy.

As his eyes swept that savage wilderness, he wondered why any man as young and ardent and sociable as Jimmy, should have buried himself in a God-forsaken land like this, away from human company and good times. That girl in his watch lived somewhere outside, out in the city country—he had been taking those furs to her. If she was his girl friend, would he have come into this North and lived here for long months without her? Hardly. He'd have brought her along. They'd have hit the trail together.

There was a possibility that this girl might be a consummate gangstress who had used Jimmy's affections to learn his secret and betray him to those killers. But he pushed the thought away from him. It clashed too violently with the charm and sweetness of that little picture.

Whatever the relationship between those two, this girl had been very precious to Jimmy—a person set apart from all the rest of the world. Jimmy had kept *her* picture when he had rid himself of every other clue to his identity; and he had paused to buy those matched silvers for her when the shadows of death were hovering over him ....

Throttling down to idle revv, he pushed the stick sharply forward and began the long glide for the Clearwater slough, where the northern planes had a pier and aërial base.

Unused to pontooned craft, he wished that this landing on the narrow slough was over with. These people at McMurray would be watching him come in; and if he sat down as clumsily as at Edmonton, his story about being a roving geologist, prospecting by air, might not get by.

Dropping down and down, out of the woolpack and through the wispy stratus below, he watched the town and slough rise up to meet him. At the railhead wharf a Hudson Bay steamer was anchored, awaiting the weekly train from Edmonton. From the slough a narrow road led back three hundred yards, through an aspen drogue, to the town itself. At the plane pier a red Bellanca was moored, a number of men were at work, and some Indians were stretched out asleep on the planking.

With a glance at the wind sock, Noel glided over the pier and on north to the Forks, kicked the Diomede around, dropped down into the slough, leveled off and headed back for the aërial base, skimming low over the water.

After an interminable minute the plane touched, smacked along on the wavelets, finally sank its heels into the current and sat down—somewhat splashily but better than he had expected.

He flicked the throttle up a notch, and taxied toward the pier on easy revv.

Two men in a motor-canoe came out to get him, towed him alongside the Bellanca; and he stepped out upon the wharf.

A lanky raw-boned man of thirty, who was directing the men at work, walked over to meet him.

"Hullo, partner," the man greeted, with a grin and friendly handclasp. "Name's Barclay. 'Strap' to you. I push a crate up and down the Three Rivers for the Alberta & Arctic Mail. What jail did you break out of and why?"

"Ontario," Noel replied. He liked this Arctic pilot, with humorous drawl and blunt honest features. "My name's Lanier. Geologist. Free-lancing. There's a sort of lull over east, so I thought I'd give this Three Rivers country a spin."

"Huh! It'll give *you* the spin! If you're heading down that God-awful drag"—he motioned into the savage North—"and if you're planning to knock around down there very long, I hope you haven't got any relations who'll miss you much."

"Is it all that bad?"

"Oh, it's not so tough right now, in summer; but Lord pity you after the ducks go south! Anything that gets out of that country for the winter has got sense. Man, you'll start your engine with a blow-torch; you'll break a ski every other take-off; and when the Big Dark shuts down, you'll fly through a soupy mixture of snow and murk and woolly-whippers right out of the devil's own den. I'm telling you!"

Noel did not disbelieve him. Something of the dangers and heavy strain of Barclay's calling rested upon the man's face—in the crowfeet under his eyes, in the thrust of his jaw, in the tense nervousness beneath his jesting manner.

Barclay glanced at the red-and-black Diomede, looked twice, then asked, somewhat puzzledly:

"Where's Jimmy, partner?"

Noel did not bat an eye, but a quiver ran through him like an electric shock. *Here was a man who knew Jimmy!* With unexpected ease, within two minutes of his landing, he had run squarely into one of Jimmy's acquaintances!

"Why," he said casually, feeling his way along with the utmost care, "Jimmy decided not to come back in just now."

"I'll bet a leg the bright lights bit him," Barclay guessed. "Two years in the far North gives a fellow a powerful hanker along that general line, and when he gets outside he starts soaking up sociability in a high, wide and handsome way. My watch against a shirt button, Jimmy met some pretty number and is going round and round faster'n a three-mile tailspin."

Noel winced at the contrast between this guess and the cruel fact that Jimmy was lying in his grave at Winnipeg; but in even tones he agreed, "Yes, I presume Jimmy did want a fling." He fished adroitly for more information. "I suppose there wasn't much 'sociability' down north at, uh, this place where he, uh——"

"Manitou," Barclay helped him out.

"Certainly, Manitou. It sort of slipped my mind."

"It would anybody's. It's just a little fly-speck of a place 'way down north in New Northumbria."

This bit of information daunted Noel. Manitou, then, had been Jimmy's center of operations. That little fur-trading post far down the mighty Mackenzie, with the Great Barrens on one side and the sub-Arctic Rockies on the other—either that post or the wilderness around it held Jimmy's secret. And there he himself would have to go.

"I say, Lanier," Barclay inquired, "has young Chantrell really signed off on hard-rocking and quit for good, or did he just lend you this Diomede for a spell?"

"I bought it from him," Noel said, taking quick note of that name. Jimmy Chantrell—the "Jimmy" was authentic, all right, but that "Chantrell" had the false ring of a name assumed. And that "hard-rocking" rang hollow too. Jimmy had been no prospector, patiently grubbing around in icy waters and picking around at outcroppings.

All this meant that Jimmy had hidden his identity from these Three Rivers people and had veiled his real business by posing as a plane prospector.

"By the way, Strap," he said confidentially, "Jimmy asked me to keep quiet about my buying his Diomede and about his staying outside. He didn't say why. Don't mention it, will you?"

"Okay. It's his business. Are you putting up here at McMurray?"

"I was thinking of hitting on north as soon as I stretch my legs and get something to eat."

"You look fagged. Better get back on top before starting down the drag. Ankle up to the Buzzard Roost. That's a rambly cabin, just this side of town, where us pilots drink our beer and pound our ears. Nobody's in but me, and I'd be glad to have someone to chew the rag with."

"Why, thanks," Noel accepted, grateful for the warm hospitality.

Barclay spoke to one of the *métis* workers. "Here, Urso. Get M'sieu Lanier's duffle and show him up the road, and tell Wong to step on that frying-pan of his. Lanier, I'll finish this job here in three shakes and be there by the time you get washed up."

With the *métis* carrying his dufflebag, Noel started up the woods road to the Roost.

As he walked along, his hand unconsciously rested on the black automatic in his pocket. His judgment, sharpened to the point of instinct, told him that some members of that pack were here at McMurray. If that red-and-black Diomede had drawn Strap Barclay's instant attention, it had also drawn theirs. *They* knew, all right, that he was ex-Inspector Irving. He felt eyes upon him, watching, waiting for his first unguarded move.

"Anyhow," he mused, "I'm making tracks with this hunt. I actually know now where Jimmy came from! It shouldn't be hard to find out what his 'pot of luck' was."

Then he thought of that savage country of which he had caught a glimpse over the nose of his plane; and his elation ebbed. Thirteen hundred miles on down across that appalling wilderness, down to the musk-ox prairies and white-wolf mountains of the sub-Arctic—that's where this hunt was taking him. And when he got there he would find himself in an unfamiliar land and way of life, alone, cut off from help, and up against this shadowy pack who had slain Jimmy.

Around nine o'clock that evening Strap Barclay came breezing into the Roost.

"Noel, you're in luck, and you've got *me* to thank for it. I'll take a can of cigarettes."

Noel looked up from studying a big government map of New Northumbria. "What's the luck, Strap?"

"I've wangled you a passenger for your hop north."

"But I don't want any passenger, man. I don't wish to be tied down——"

"You'll want *this* passenger, all right! I'd have wangled this job for myself, only—damn all!—I've got to *hyak* over to Lesser Slave tomorrow, and then clean up a bunch of fur shipments along the Liard. She'll pay for your gas and oil on the trip, and that's your big item."

"*She*—?"

"Sure, a girl. And if you don't say she's a work of art, I'll eat my parka. She was Miss Canada three years ago, and she hasn't lost any ground since. To have her sitting right beside you for thirteen hundred miles and talking to you and looking at you with those eyes—say, fellow, you owe me *two* cans of cigarettes!"

Noel pushed back his chair and stood up. "See here, Strap, I'm taking no girl down north with me. Get that straight. I've got several reasons, but one is enough—on a trip like that they're an unmitigated nuisance."

"She isn't that kind a bit. She's as good a man as you or me. I flew her in from Edmonton last week, and she took that 'dry hop' like a soldier."

"There's simply nothing doing."

"Don't turn her down," Strap pleaded. "She's hung around here several days already; she'll be here till Friday, waiting for the H-B boat to pull out; then she'll be hung up again at the Big Portage at Fort James, making connections with the *Midnight Sun*. She'll waste maybe a month getting down to Manitou, when you could have her there tomorrow evening, slicker'n a whistle."

"Manitou?" That hooked Noel's interest. "She's going to Manitou?"

"Sure! That's why it's such a bang-up arrangement. She's going, you're going, she'll pay for the gas, you push the crate, and *zzppp!*—you're there!"

"Who is she?" Noel demanded. A city girl, heading for that distant post in the North, where he himself was going, where Jimmy had lived, where likely that gang had their rendezvous—was this merely coincidence?

"Her name's Harla DeLong," Strap informed. "She's connected with the Indian Bureau at Ottawa, and she's going north to do some research work on a tribe of queer Smokies. She's got to get there and get that work done and get out, all before snow flies. What d'ya say, fellow—taking her?"

Noel stood silent, thinking. Harla DeLong, of the Indian Bureau—hadn't he once traded letters with her on that Indian funds investigation? DeLong, Harla—that was the name, all right. As he remembered, she edited the Indian language publications of the Bureau and wrote technical treatises on the prehistoric migrations from Asia to America.

But he had imagined her as an oldish person, wearing horn-rimmed glasses; and Strap's description of her as young and "a work of art" aroused his suspicion. *Maybe* this girl was Harla

DeLong. And maybe she was an impostor, using that name and reputation for a purpose.

"I'll talk to her, Strap," he agreed, cautiously. "Where'll I find her?"

"She's staying at Mrs. Tooley's Lodging, but just now she's down the street where you hear that shooting. I'd take you over and introduce you, only I've got to go and inspect my Bellank for an early hop-off."

When Strap was gone, Noel picked up his hat, left the Roost and started up the road to the hamlet.

It was well after nine in the evening, but the sun still lingered above the northwest horizon, touching the aspen hills to a mellow golden. He was thankful for that lingering sun. In his situation daylight was a good friend, and he was glad there would be only four hours of twilight and dark.

When he reached the edge of town, he stopped on the slab walk for a careful look up and down the street.

The general stores, the false-front buildings, the smell of leather and wood-smoke, the swart Crees and half-breeds loafing along the walks, gave a rough-and-ready frontier tone to the little settlement. Through this historic post, in the decades past, had flowed the rushes to the Norman Oil and the Great Bear and even a few trickles of the Klondike hegira; it had lived through its own Tar Sand boom and the delirious excitement of getting a railroad; but it still retained a flavor of the old voyageur days when the Montrealers had embarked, down at that slough, in their forty-foot canoes, and had come back, a year or two later, with their *paquetons* of precious peltry from the Tierre Inconnu to the north.

In front of the stores little knots of trappers and prospectors were smoking, talking. In the center of the broad street a number of large wolfish huskies were cruising up and down, assiduously looking for a good free-for-all fight. At a clapboard building a hundred yards north a "shanty dance" was starting up, catching its music from an Edmonton station.

Just this side of the dance several dozen men were gathered in a vacant lot; at intervals came the sharp *p-ll-ink* of a small-bore rifle; and after each shot a hubbub of excitement burst from the crowd.

Realizing that this was the shooting which Strap had referred to, Noel crossed the street and approached the gathering, with ears and eyes alert.

As he reached the fringe of the crowd he saw that a rifle match, beloved in this North where the rifle was the weapon par excellence, was being staged. Some demonstrator for an arms company, traveling the Three Rivers to sell guns and ammunition, had set up his small portable gallery and challenged "one and all" to outshoot him.

An elimination match, starting out with nearly twenty crack shots competing, the contest had boiled down to a locked battle between two people.

One of those two was the deadly-shooting demonstrator. The other—— As Noel edged his way into the crowd, he saw with astonishment that the other finalist was this girl of whom he was in quest.

Facing the target-box forty feet away, she was carefully greasing a cartridge, slipping it into the single-shot rifle and closing the bolt. Medium tall, graceful of body, with a lance-like erectness about her, she was clad in a belted suit of blue corduroy, and small laced boots. Her hair was black and silken; and when she moved, the slant sun-rays shimmered and danced in it like soft golden fires.

He could not see her face; but her shapely head and the proud poise of it brought him, for some intangible reason, a vivid memory of handsome young Jimmy as the latter had sat by the desk with the light flooding down upon his head and shoulders.

She lifted the rifle and called, "Ready!" The man operating the target-box called back:

> "The woodpecker flies from tree to tree;
> If you plunk him down you're better'n me."

Against the black background of the target a small white object appeared, and started across the stage with the wavy undulating motion of a woodpecker's flight.

The girl squeezed the trigger. *P-ll-ink!* The metal object flopped over.

The crowd milled and applauded, plainly rooting for the girl to win. Even her opponent, the demonstrator, was wholeheartedly backing her. An artist with guns and gun-work, he was fired to zeal by fine shooting, regardless of who was doing it or who won.

"Steady, girl, steady," he encouraged, swabbing the rifle and handing it back. "Pipe down and keep quiet, you fellows. Two more shots, Miss DeLong, and you'll draw me; and b'Lord there's no man from here to Aklavik can do the same."

The girl turned around and asked for a cartridge from the man who was proudly holding her cartridge box; and Noel had full view of her face. In spite of his usual cold steadiness he jerked a little, and for moments he could only stare at her. The same black eyes and hair; the same nose, lips, throat; the same and identical person beyond the ghost of a doubt... *There stood the girl whose picture Jimmy had carried in his watch!*

CHAPTER FOUR

THE shooting went on. Noel paid no attention. A host of questions were racing through his mind like an avalanche sweep. Was this girl really Harla DeLong of the Indian Bureau, or an impostor? Did she know Jimmy's baffling secret? Did she know those killers? And why was she going to Manitou?

The girl lifted the rifle again. "Ready!" The man called back:

"The grizzly b'ar can hug you in two;
You better git him er he'll git you."

Across the target-stage moved a diminutive bear-shaped object. Its jerky baffling motion did somewhat suggest the humpy gait of a lumbering silvertip.

P-ll-ink! The "bear" fell down.

As the crowd jostled and gaped, Noel edged around where he could observe the girl better. Her talent with a rifle and her camaraderie with these rough tobacco-chewing men made her seem like a bad case of tomboy—more familiar with gun and fly-pole than with a tea-urn, and quite the person to take a two-hundred-mile "dry hop" without fidgeting.

She looked to be twenty-six or twenty-seven—several years older than when that snapshot had been taken. She seemed a bit more mature, too; but he fancied that behind that veneer of steadiness she was still the same impetuous and vitally alive girl of that little photograph. She was indeed lovely; her face and figure, the light in her black eyes, the delicate molding of her features, made him agree wholeheartedly with Strap's ecstatic description of her.

Even before he had seen her face he had been all but sure of her relationship to Jimmy; and now, as he studied her, noticing the unmistakable resemblance not only of features but of mannerisms and poise and gesture, his last doubt vanished. This girl was Jimmy's older sister.

He was profoundly glad of this discovery. It meant that she was no gangstress but a person of good heart and conscience. As he had hoped. In his Mounted years he had seen all of evil and disillusionment that he wanted to see.

Her last and crucial target came up. A small snake wiggling sinuously across the stage, it was an almost impossible shot, at that distance; and she missed it.

The crowd groaned. The demonstrator urged her: "Take another try! These bozos flustered you. Go on, shoot again!"

The girl refused point-blank. "No, no. I wasn't disturbed a bit. I missed clean. You licked me, and that's that." And she shook hands with him in congratulation.

"She takes defeat like a good sport," Noel thought. And as she began chatting with Strap's mechanic and a Mounted constable, he noticed how well she could mix with people; how natural and easy she was. He envied her for that. Like Jimmy, she had the priceless knack of friendship.

Presently she happened to look his way and see him. As though realizing that he was not one of this ordinary crowd, she gave him a long searching glance. He stepped up.

As he confronted her and their glances met, Noel found himself looking into the blackest eyes he had ever seen. They were so clear and steady—he could well understand why she could look down a rifle barrel with the best of these men. Friendly eyes, they were; friendly toward him.

Though she and he had not yet spoken, in her attitude there was a certain respect such as she had not shown toward these others. She seemed to sense that he was of different metal.

He said to her: "I'm Lanier. Strap Barclay mentioned me, didn't he?"

"Yes," she replied, in clear low-pitched voice. "He told me that you're flying down north to Manitou, Mr. Lanier."

"I'm heading north, true," Noel parried, "but whether and when I'll get to Manitou is a question."

A keen disappointment flitted across her face. "But—but I thought … Strap said you were going for sure. I'd like awf'ly to get down north just as quickly as possible, Mr. Lanier. If you're planning to go anywhere at all within striking distance of Manitou, maybe we can hit on some arrangement."

"Maybe we can," Noel agreed. In order to get better acquainted with this girl and find out how much she knew about her brother's grim feud, he suggested, "Shall we step into the drug store for a drink, and talk this over?"

"Let's do." With an engaging smile she added, "After the trouncing I just got I need some consolation; and a chocolate soda, with whipped cream on top, and a red cherry on the tippest top—that's a secret weakness of mine."

They went down the board walk and into the drug store. With twilight coming on and the store a bit dim, Noel took the precaution of sitting so that he had a good solid wall at his back and could also watch the door. Though he had failed to catch one suspicious word or glance here at McMurray, he knew that the death which had struck Jimmy down was hovering over himself now, claiming him as its next. To walk in the glare of an unseen spotlight while his enemies were hidden in the dark of anonymity—it was a bit blood-chilling.

"Strap tells me," he led off, after ordering their sodas, "that you're going north to do field work on some Tenneh tribe, Miss DeLong."

"Oh, no, not Tenneh!" she objected. "A band called the Dinokuis. They don't belong to the Tenneh race at all. They're 'tall' Indians, not short spindly Tennehs. They're a very primitive and puzzling band, living in the mountains northwest of Manitou."

"Never heard of them," Noel said, watching a stray wisp of hair that lay against her cheek. How long her lashes were! And how silken her hair! A girl of her charm and witchery, writing dusty studies on Indian languages and loping the bush to study tribes *au naturel*—it just didn't seem possible.

"Few people have heard of them," the girl replied. "To most folk they're just another tribe of 'Smokies'; but to anthropologists they're an engrossing riddle. What little we know about them indicates that they were a part of an ancient migration wave from Asia. For some reason they didn't come on south; they got stuck in the North, got isolated in a mountain refuge, and there they are today."

Forgetting all about her soda, she went on, enthusiastically: "If I can get down there to them, Mr. Lanier, I'm going to do that research job brown! I've got recording disks to take down their speech; I'll get their old Asiatic legends; I'll make a scientific collection of their artifacts. If you could step back across the centuries, walk into an ancient Mound-builder village, watch them at work, talk to them, sit in at their ceremonies—that's just about what a person will be doing when he visits these Dinokuis."

As Noel listened, his doubts about her being Harla DeLong, of the Indian Bureau, solwly ebbed and vanished. She *was* Harla DeLong. A clever-tongued person might fake this technical language, but no impostor could fake this enthusiastic zeal. That was genuine.

"Well," he thought, "here's another big step. Jimmy's name was Jimmy DeLong." He recalled those harassed days in Winnipeg when he had hunted desperately and almost hopelessly for the slightest clue on this case. Now he knew the name and wilderness home of his strange young visitor; and here in this dim drug store he was looking across a soda table at Jimmy's own sister.

But why was Harla going down to Manitou? That was a puzzler. Beyond question she did wish to study those queer Indians. But if that was her sole reason for this sub-Arctic trip, why hadn't she gone in at the spring break-up instead of now, when so few open weeks remained?

"Pardon me," he interposed, after she had talked for five straight minutes about those Dinokuis, "but you'd better attack that 'secret weakness' of yours before it goes flat. Here"—and he handed her one of his straws; she had unthinkingly crumpled both of hers in her eager description of that ancient band.

The music from the dance came drifting into the store. The sun still was gliding the tops of the aspen hills, but the purple shadows of owl-dusk were beginning to settle over the little hamlet. Uneasy, Noel glanced out at the street. That woods road down to the Roost would be a dark gantlet for him unless he went back at once. But first he had to decide about taking Harla DeLong to Manitou.

He made himself look away from her, to blank out the pleasantness of her company; and on coldly rational lines he weighed the pro's and con's of taking her along. He was on a man-hunt, the most dangerous he had ever tackled. He was up against a pack of shadows who killed and laughed and faded. To nail them was the job in hand, and that came first. Harla might clutter up his hunt, unless he kept her absolutely in the dark about himself.

He believed he could do this. If he could, she would be of great help to him at Manitou. Undoubtedly she knew Something about Jimmy's venture and likely something about those men too. On the long flight and at the little Mackenzie post he could get invaluable leads from her. If he went by himself he might have to pry and poke around for a fortnight or a month to get the facts he needed. And those men would not let him live that long. He would have to strike swift and hard.

He looked at her again. "About this Manitou trip, Miss DeLong," he said slowly, aware that his decision was fraught with consequences both for himself and for Harla. "I was planning to head for Reliance, but I can just as well go to Manitou first; and since it's important for you to get there quickly, I'll be very glad to take you."

"Oh, gee!" She reached across the table impulsively and clasped his hand. "That's awf'ly good of you. A thirteen-hundred-mile lift! If you knew how badly I want to get there you'd know how grateful I am."

"Not at all. The other way around. As a matter of fact, Strap charged me two cans of cigarettes for merely telling me that you wanted to go down the Three Rivers."

"He did?"

"Yes, and I consider that he sold the tip at a ridiculously cheap price."

"Sold down the river, for two cans of cigarettes," Harla mused; and they both laughed.

Several times, as they attended to the sodas and talked about the long wilderness flight ahead, Noel observed that Harla was looking at him in an odd questioning way, as though she found it hard to believe that he was a knockabout prospector, wasting his years on the fringe of the mining game. He cautioned himself: "Be careful with this girl. She's keen; she'll see through you, and the devil will be to pay then."

Presently Harla remarked: "That's a shanty dance up the walk, Mr. Lanier. Shanty dances are usually great fun. I was raised in northern Ontario, at a trading post, and we used to dance the rafters off every time enough people came in."

For a moment Noel hardly knew what to say. He himself was in little mood for dancing, with worries and dangers gathering around him like the gathering twilight outside. But Harla wanted to go up there. She had said so, as plainly as she could. And she wanted *him* to take her. Over all these other men she had given him preference.

With a recklessness that was alien to him ordinarily, he decided to take her up to that dance, and danger be damned. He could get back to the Roost somehow, afterward. As excuse to his conscience he told himself that if he spent this evening with her he would pick up a lot worth knowing.

At the dance hall an hour later, as they steered themselves clear of heavy-booted prospectors and clumsy *métis* couples, Harla commented:

"You seem to be expecting company, Noel."

"Why, what makes you say that, girl?"

"You've been watching this crowd and the door and even the windows as though—I don't know just what."

"Habit," Noel jested, a little alarmed at her keenness. "You see, I used to be a bouncer at a dance hall and had to keep on the lookout for trouble——"

"I don't believe that. You haven't been near a dance hall in moons and moons."

"Am I all that bad?"

"Not now. You've picked up wonderfully fast."

They bumped into a *métis* couple who were standing in the middle of the floor and jumping up and down. With a nod of apology and a smile at each other they swung into the rhythm again.

Over in the doorway Noel saw Strap's handy-man, Urso Goulet, and Urso's brother, Hannibal, staring at him in queer fashion. From anyone else that stare would have put him on guard; but by no stretch of the imagination could those simple-hearted *métis* be members of that pack. He knew this positively, and gave them no further thought.

Though he had picked up little from Harla, he was glad he had come to this dance. Against his background of lonely evenings and human lonesomeness, the hour had been unexpectedly pleasant and sunlit. With surprise, almost with astonishment, he was aware that Harla instinctively liked him, as Jimmy had. In the past several months, broke and lonely and in disgrace, there had been times when he felt that he had completely lost the human touch. That his years as a mere name and number had put a blight upon him. That he belonged to the cold world of shadows. Now he could believe that this was not so. At least it was not true with Harla DeLong.

When he glanced at the doorway again, the two Goulet *métis* were gone, but Strap Barclay was standing there. After a moment or two the pilot stepped in through the crowd and planted himself squarely in front of them. They had to stop.

"So!" Strap snorted, eying Noel scornfully. "Are you the fellow that told me, down at the Roost, that a girl was an unmitigated nuisance?—and here you are, fantasticating with her! Miss Harla, he swore up and down that for all he cared you could start for Manitou in a rowboat, or stick here till freezing weather and skate down on the ice; and then he turns around and monopolizes you all evening!

"Now see here, Miss Harla, it was really me that promoted you this trip—oh, he's taking you, all right; don't need to tell *me*—and how about my rake-off? Besides that, you ought to look ahead. After he gets you down north he'll bust his neck down there somewhere, and I'll be the one to fly you back out. You ought to think about that. There's only a couple or three dances left, and do I get 'em or don't I?"

"Really, Strap," Harla tried to put him off, "I've got to get some sleep tonight. We're leaving McMurray very early so that we'll be sure to make Manitou tomorrow."

"Sleep? In this country people do all their sleeping in the winter time, like a bear, and stay up all summer. Talk about daylight savings—city people don't know nothing! And what's the difference if you don't make Manitou all in one drag? You can do like the Swede jumping across the crick—make it in two yumps."

Harla looked at Noel.

"Do you mind? He really does rate a dance or two even if he did sell me down the river."

Noel glanced through the window at the deep dark outside. In a short while this dance would end. If he was here Harla would naturally expect him to walk home with her.

He shouldn't do that. It would expose her to danger. But if she went with Strap she would be entirely safe.

"I do mind," he said, "but I feel that I owe Strap something, considering that he was your and my catalytic agent."

"What's that?" Strap demanded. "Say, I'm going to look that jaw-breaker up in a dictionary, and if it's as bad a slam as it sounds like, I'll dump some nitroglycerin into that gas tank of yours." He took possession of Harla and started dancing. "Go on and scram," he ordered Noel, over his shoulder. "Go on home and pound your ear."

Noel exchanged a glance of "Good night" with Harla, and walked over to the door.

In spite of the late hour the stores were still lighted, and the knots of loiterers had thinned but little. The lights and the people made him feel safe, for the present. Those enemies were altogether too cagey to strike at him within eye-witness of half a hundred men.

Before stepping outside upon the walk, he glanced back, at Harla and Strap. As he watched them dancing, a suspicion which had been growing on him ever since his talk with Harla in the drug store, mounted to an absolute certainty. Whatever her purpose in making this four-thousand-mile trip from Ottawa to that pot of trouble down in the sub-Arctic, Harla DeLong knew nothing whatsoever about that murder in Winnipeg and had not the remotest idea that Jimmy was not alive. At the rifle match, over the soda, at this dance, she had laughed and chatted light-heartedly.

A sensitive girl, sensitive to joy and sorrow, she would never have done that, with her brother less than a week dead. It was unthinkable.

However much she wanted to study those Dinokui Indians. her chief purpose was to visit Jimmy and be with him for a time.

Manitou, he mused, in heartfelt pity, was going to be a tragic trail-end for her. Eagerly and confidently she was expecting to meet her brother at that little fur post on the Mackenzie; but instead of that she was going to find only silence—the silent oblivion into which Jimmy had vanished and from which he would never return.

CHAPTER FIVE

FROM the doorway Noel glanced down the street to the corner where the woods road branched off. It was only a long stone's throw from that corner down to the Roost. He was tempted to risk it.

But premonition whispered warning. Death had hit Jimmy like quick lightning; and those two hundred yards might well be his own death walk.

After some careful planning, he strolled across the street to a clump of pines and faded into their shadows. Flattened against a tree, he waited there for several minutes, making sure that no one had followed him away from the dance. Then he eased on deeper into the clump, reached the edge of the aspen drogue and headed straight down through the woods for the Roost, avoiding that road altogether.

A blood-red moon, just edging above the hills across the Clearwater, had started up the wolves. From here and there, far back in the surrounding wilderness, their long-drawn wailing came drifting into the valley. Ahead of him an Arctic owl hooted its weird eleven-noted call. As he passed a deerbush thicket he was startled by a quick *pad-pad-pad*, like the footsteps of those men who had killed Jimmy; and he had an unpleasant second before realizing that the noise was only the stamping of a buck rabbit.

"Damn these woods!" he swore wearily. He was tired; the strain of constant alertness had made his nerves jumpy; the strange sounds and shadows of the dark drogue preyed on his imagination. He wished he were back in the city, matching himself against a city gang. A gang even like Frank Rocco's would be a positive relief compared to these outlanders.

He was troubled, too, about Harla's safety. Harla was in danger, in this Three Rivers country. This uncanny pack knew who she was. They were watching her, just as they were watching him. So long as she was no menace to them, they probably would leave her alone. But the instant she put them in any sort of jeopardy, that outfit would "take care" of her. He himself, a man and a trained professional with years of experience, stood a chance to keep alive. But Harla was a girl, totally without training, totally defenseless except for what protection he himself could throw around her.

Above all things, he had to keep her from learning anything about Jimmy's death. Of headlong passionate nature, she would fly to pieces if she knew about that. She entirely lacked the caution and discipline and grim patience necessary on this job. She would break all out of control, go gunning for those men herself—and get killed.

The music from the dance came sifting down through the silent woods, and as he listened to it he wished himself back there—with Harla. He could still feel her arm about him, her breath upon his cheek; and on his jacket sleeve lingered a touch of perfume—some strange flower odor that was totally new to him.

In ten minutes he came out to the edge of the small Roost clearing. The building was dark, the clearing apparently empty; but he stopped to scout the place out.

A curious tapping sound from the front porch of the cabin puzzled him for a moment; but then he heard the rattle of a dog's collar, and the puzzle cleared up. Big Yuke, Strap's huge watchdog, was scratching himself.

"With that brute on guard," he thought, "no strangers are prowling around within nose-shot of this place." He crossed the clearing and stepped around to the front. "Hello, Yuke. Are the fleas staging a shanty dance on you tonight?"

Inside the screen porch the big dog got up, shook himself and keened in friendly way. Perhaps remembering that this man outside had given him a juicy caribou collop that afternoon and picked bothersome sand-burrs out of his ears, he pawed against the netting and tail-wagged a welcome.

Noel walked on toward the porch.

As he came within three steps of the door, a dark figure leaped up, with magic suddenness, from behind a low rick of wood, and swung a murderous blow at his head with a heavy club, a five-foot length of spike-studded scantling.

The attack broke upon Noel so quickly that he could only fling up his arm, instinctively, to protect himself. The swishing blow, deflected an inch or two, crashed against his right shoulder, staggering him, knocking the black automatic from his hand. The scantling slid down his right arm, its spikes ripping through his jacket and shirt like hot claws.

As he reeled backward, groggy and weaponless, a second man leaped from behind a rain-spout hogshead, brandishing a long-bladed skinning knife. A third, hidden behind an old fur press, sprang out and came lunging at Noel, growling some inarticulate bush-French oath.

They were all three powerful and thick-set men. From their oaths and their blind headlong rush, they seemed crazed with anger, with lust to kill. They were snarling like animals as they came at him.

With his eyes on that evilly glinting steel, Noel seized a stick of wood from the rick, backed up another step, whipped up the stick and flung it with all his strength at the enemy with the knife.

The whizzing stob caught the man a smashing blow across the forehead, stopped his lunge, knocked him so cold that he sprawled face downward in the wood chips and lay there twitching.

Even in those tumultuous moments Noel was aware, in a flash-quick way, that his berserk attempt to kill him was a clumsy and ill-planned attempt, totally unlike that clean deadly strike at Jimmy; totally unlike anything he had expected from those shadows.

The man from behind the fur press grappled with him and tried to topple him to the ground. Tearing free, Noel grabbed for another stob and whirled to meet that first enemy, who was rushing at him with the scantling arched back for a swing. One blow from that scantling, studded with those six-inch spikes, would brain a person.

In the blind fury of his charge the man stumbled over a chopping block and fell to his knees.

"Urso!" he yelled at the unconscious man on the ground. "Get op! Dat knife—slash heem! Keel heem."

The cry told Noel who his assailants were. Urso Goulet and Urso's brother and some other half-breed!

Astounded and bewildered, he backed up, to get away from them and stop the fight before somebody got killed. They had made a mistake, had mistaken him for someone else. This was no strike from those enemies. These half-breeds, slow-minded, dull and heavy—members of that pack? Preposterous. They hadn't wits enough to chop wood for those outlanders.

"Stop it!" he cried at them. "You idiots, I'm Lanier! Drop those——"

"We drop you!" the man with scantling rasped. "We keel you!" He leaped up and lunged at Noel again.

On the porch big Yuke had jumped to the door, when the fight had first broken open, and had pawed at the latch. But the latch had held. Now, snarling savagely, the dog backed up against the wall, crouched and then flung himself at the screen—a hundred and fifty pounds of caged fury. With a rip he tore through the netting as though it was so much paper, and sprawled heavily on the ground outside.

For a second, as the fearsome animal scrambled up and crouched again, Noel thought that the dog was going to come at him. He was quickly set right. Before the man with the scantling could whirl around, the huge husky sprang upon him, toppled him over against the rick and slashed at his throat.

"Yuke!" Noel cried, springing in. Fittingly he caught a glimpse of the third man whirling away and melting into the dark. "Here, Yuke! Down!"

He seized Yuke by the collar, dragged him off the man, pinioned the dog with his legs, wound both hands into the leather collar and choked off Yuke's wind. "You, there"—to the man on hands and knees—"get up, get away from here. I can't hold this dog if his collar slips. He'll tear your throat out. Clear away!"

In a whimpering panic the man scrambled up and headed for the dark road; and only Urso Goulet was left, lying there unconscious in the wood chips....

Inside the cabin Noel bathed the dirt and blood from Urso's face, forced a sip of water between his lips and worked with him till finally he had the 'breed sitting up, groggy and wander-witted.

Noel brought him a cup of black coffee laced with brandy. "Here. Drink this. How d'you feel—anything bad wrong?"

The 'breed struck at Noel's hand and dashed the cup to the floor.

"*Chien,* you!" he growled feebly, glaring at Noel with unmistakable hatred. "Don' touch me. I have despise for you."

"All right, if that's how you feel about it. But you're going to talk to me, you'll answer some questions for me, or I'll hammer it out of you."

He drew the window blinds, locked the door, came back. His shoulder and arm were stinging badly, and the blood from those spike weals was trickling to his fingertips; but he was unmindful of that. This unprovoked attempt to murder him was a mystery worth digging into. These pious and simple-minded Goulets, common laborers and wood-choppers here at McMurray, were no criminals, no members of that pack or even on the outermost fringe of it.

Yet the fact remained that they had tried to kill him. Something had exploded their usual stolid piety. Something had set them ablaze and unleashed all the blood-fury of their Indian heritage.

"Who was that other man out there, Urso?" he demanded of the sullen *métis*. "I mean, besides Hannibal."

"I don' tell you nut'ing."

"You'd better! You tried to kill me. For that the Mounted Police will take you away from McMurray, take you away off and put you in a big stone pen. But if you talk to me, and talk straight—— Who was that other man?"

"Riel."

"Who's he?"

"Riel Roberval. He is ongaged to Mareea."

"Who's Mareea?"

The question struck fire from the half-breed. He stood up, swaying groggily, and shook a fist at Noel.

"You know plenty good who Mareea is! W'y you tell all dem damn-dirty lies 'bout Mareea? 'Bout how you go walk in dat aspen *bois* wit' Mareea. 'Bout how you do dis and dat wit' Mareea. You liar, Mareea is *good* girl! But dem Ind'ans op dere, and all dese *métis*, dey be'lieve w'at you said. Ever'body w'ispering and snick-ering 'bout Mareea. She go home, cry. She ruin'. Riel Roberval, he say he not marry her now——"

"Wait a minute," Noel interrupted. "In the name of *le bon Dieu*, who is this Mareea?"

"Don' you try to lie out of dis! You won' spread dem lies 'bout my leetle seester and den make s'prised face and say you don' know nut'ing 'bout it."

"Your sister? Mareea?" Noel groped. "*I* spread lies about her? Have you gone crazy, fellow? I never knew you had a sister. Till you mentioned her I never heard of Mareea. How on earth could I talk about a person that I didn't even know existed?"

"I t'ink you lie," Urso asserted, but with less vehemence.

"Look here—who told you that I said these things about Mareea?"

"Lot of pipple. It go 'round *buzz-buzz*. Ever'body talk 'bout it."

"This *buzz-buzz* was a lie. Somebody lied about me. Answer my question: *Who started that rumor?*"

"I—I don' know," the *métis* stammered. "If you didn' say dem t'ings, I don' unnerstan' how dis talk got start'."

"Well, *I'm* beginning to 'unnerstand,' " Noel said, flipping the blood from his hand. Those enemies had struck at him. Not with knife or bullet but in a subtler way. Rather than run any risk by getting him themselves, they had used these poor ignorant half-breeds as their tool. They had pumped these *métis* full of inflammable lies and touched a match to the three of them—Urso, Hannibal and this Riel Roberval.

They certainly knew half-breed nature to its depths, those men. They had pressed the one button which could rouse these stolid Goulets to fury. And their move had nearly worked. It was plain luck that he had not been killed out there a few minutes ago.

Pretty brainy, their attempt. Brainy and heartless. In order to rub him out they had launched a move that would have taken three innocent men to the gallows.

Urso pressed his hands against his aching head. "Dis been awful opset night. I go crazy out dere, I guess." He looked up at Noel, trembly and afraid. "W'at you go to do wit' me? I don' min' dat pen for myself, but Hannibal, my yo'ng brutter, and Riel——"

"Forget it," Noel bade, pitying him. "Go on home, Urso. You weren't to blame for this. Only, the next time you try to kill somebody, be sure you've got the right man."

When the *métis* had trudged out, he pulled off his jacket and shirt and began plastering up his arm and shoulder. As he worked he thought, grimly: "Well, I've contacted them, I lured them into an overt act, all right—but that's all the good it did me." From back in the shadows they had struck at him, in deadly way, and he knew no more about them now than before.

With something of fright he remembered Jimmy's words to him in distant Winnipeg: "They're so—so damned ghostlike. You can't see 'em, can't fight 'em; you just know they're there and they've got you on the spot."

CHAPTER SIX

D OWN at the Clearwater pier, early the next morning, Noel carefully inspected the little Diomede, made sure it had not been tampered with, stowed away his baggage and Harla's, and pumped the floats dry.

Then he started tanking the ship for the long flight.

For Harla's own sake he wished that she were safely back in Ottawa, four thousand miles away. She had no protection save what he could give her, and his company was terrifically dangerous. At their first chance those unknowns were going to strike at him again, in some ruthless unexpected fashion; and the lightning bolt crackling out of the sky at him might catch Harla too.

In order to make the long flight at one hop, he tanked the Diomede to capacity, seventy gallons—all that the little ship could get off the water with. If he was in the air all the way from McMurray to Manitou, those men would have little chance to launch calamity at him, and so Harla would be safe.

While he was rolling the empty drums back to the pier shed, Harla came down the trail, carrying her light .25-35 rifle and a creel of food for the trip. The slant sun of three o'clock was spangling her hair; and she was wearing a little cluster of fire-flowers which she had picked along that woods road.

"Hello, Noel," she greeted him, with a warmth that set his pulse hammering. "I'm sorry to be so late."

He had to smile at the sleepiness in her black eyes. "You're right on time, girl. I'm just now ready."

"But that's the point; I wanted to help you get ready——"

She broke off, her eyes opened widely; and Noel, following her glance, saw that she was staring at the little Diomede. A quiver of misgiving shot through him. Did she know whose plane this had been?

"That ship there—that Diomede—where'd you get that?" she demanded.

"Winnipeg," Noel said casually, wiping a smudge of oil from his fingers.

"You mean you bought it? From whom?"

"I bought it new."

Harla looked at him, a sharp searching glance; and in her eyes Noel saw a nameless suspicion. Jimmy evidently had written her about his new "crate," describing it with all the pride of ownership; and now, suddenly confronted with a craft that tallied exactly, she was thunderstruck.

"A Diomede," she breathed, "red and black, three-place, radial, and even ruddered floats...I didn't imagine there were two such planes in the whole Dominion!"

"There are dozens," Noel lied, fighting against that suspicion of hers. "This particular job is popular with timber and mining men. It's light on gas, and swift; and that red-and-black color is highly conspicuous, especially against snow. When you have a forced landing in country like this, it's well to be so conspicuous that searching planes can spot you a long way off."

Harla nodded, but her smile did not come back. Hard hit by the sight of the little ship, she moved over to the pier edge and laid her hand on the wing of the craft, as though by touching it she might tell whether it was Jimmy's plane, her brother's trim Diomede.

As Noel stowed her rifle in the ceiling rack and untied the mooring ropes, he swore at his luck. Harla's suspicion packed dynamite, for himself and his hunt both. If she ever discovered that he had any connection at all with Jimmy, he would have to start explaining. That would be fatal to his hunt and probably fatal to her.

He hated to get tangled in a mass of lies and evasions. Already he was on shaky ground with her. Last night she had had her doubts about his being a prospector. Now she had her suspicions about this plane. What would come next heaven alone knew.

And he was helpless to defend himself. That was the worst of it. He dared not tell her one word of the truth.

He swung the Diomede away from the pier, cranked the inertia, climbed into the cabin beside Harla; and they started out upon the slough. After jockeying around in mid-channel till the motor was warm and smooth, he headed the Diomede up stream, gunned the plane, and went skimming up toward a willow island a mile south.

Aided by a stiff breeze and slapping waves, the Diomede climbed onto the step easily enough, but it balked at taking the jump. Heavily laden with gas and baggage, it skimmed along bumpily through the whitecaps; but its pontoon heels clung to the water stubbornly.

The willow island loomed up closer and closer. Though the little plane was rearing like a bronco, Noel screwed another round out of the stabilizer and pumped still harder at the stick. Unless he tore free he would have to taxi back and dump part of the gas. That meant landing at Fort Northumbria. And that meant danger to Harla.

Just as he was reaching to throttle down, a heavy wave and a lucky gust of wind struck at the same instant; the Diomede bounced into the air, roared over the willow island; and the river and valley began falling away.

Circling over McMurray, he climbed swiftly to eight thousand feet, and then headed into the North.

The morning was bright and sunlit. Around and above them fields of woolpack hung against the blue sky like inverted lakes of purest white. The air was so clear that far westward, a full hundred miles away, the foothills of the Rockies rose out of the pearl-gray haze of great distance.

"Comfortable?" he asked Harla, above the engine thrum.

"Yes, thanks," she said, and was silent again.

In the inclinometer glass her face was mirrored plainly, and he watched her. Again and again she turned her head and surreptitiously studied him, as though asking, "Who *are* you?" She had little to say. Back here on the Clearwater pier she had changed like a shift of wind to the north. Her warm friendliness of last evening had turned to silence and a questioning suspicion.

He could not blame her for drawing away from him. He *had* lied about himself, and this was her brother's very plane she was riding in. But still, after their happy evening and dance, he was wounded by her coldness. This flight with her, to which he had looked forward so eagerly, was bitterly disappointing; and Manitou promised to be even worse.

Fifty miles north of McMurray he turned and glanced back along their route, on the lookout for an enemy plane. Unquestionably that shadowy outfit had aircraft. Without planes they could never have followed Jimmy out of the North.

He saw nothing. The cloud fields and the open sky were empty.

Unable to strike up any talk with Harla, he gave his attention to the strange country into which they were penetrating. Except for a few timbered backbones of Laurentian shield-rock, the whole vast panorama to the north and east was a flat waterlogged muskeg.

Small wonder, he thought, that the old Montrealers had called their fur expeditions into this Three Rivers country not "travels" or "treks" but "voyages."

An hour and a half after leaving McMurray he sighted Lake Athabasca, a great dull-colored water dotted with pretty pine islands. With a glance at the strip map on the wall, he veered a few points eastward, away from the regular plane route, to avoid

Fort Chipewyan. If any enemy ship was on the lookout for them there, it would dog them up across the latitudes clear to Manitou.

Slowly the island-studded Athabasca swam nearer, and the Diomede finally sailed out above its broad expanse. Keeping out of sight of Chipewyan Noel flew on across the great lake, reached the north shore, passed over a broad river delta, and crossed a rocky watershed between the Athabasca and Slave drainage systems.

North of that watershed he came into the Grand Marais— the wildest, loneliest, weirdest region he had ever seen or imagined.

He had thought the Athabasca muskeg about the last word in the way of marsh country; but now it seemed a mere frog-swamp compared to this watery wilderness of the Grand Marais. Cut by a thousand channels and stagnant sloughs and slow rivers that coiled and tangled like a mass of snakes; glistening everywhere with lakes and chains of lakes a patch-work of slimy-green muskeg and flag fields and quivering gray bog—it was a fearsome region, a strange amphibious country that was neither land nor water.

Uninhabitable to man, with his guns and traps and poison, the territory was a sanctuary for muskrat, mink, beaver, otter; and it looked huge enough to be rookery grounds for all the waterfowl of a continent.

As Noel gazed down at the bottomless muskeg and miry lakes, the thought of a forced landing made him flinch. He was far east of the Slave River, the usual air route; and search planes would not know where to hunt. Across that oozy muskeg down there he and Harla could not foot-slog a mile a day; and the mosquito hordes and vicious *brûlé* flies would pull them down like a legion of tiny blood-thirsty wolves.

But if he jogged over and followed the Slave, his enemies might pick him up, swoop upon him along some lonely reach, and shoot him out of the air.

Of the two dangers, the country and that pack, he chose the country.

To break the monotony for Harla, who was getting tired and restless, he suggested: "Would you like to spell me for a way? Strap told me that you handle a stick quite well."

Harla was all eagerness. "I'd like to, lots. I love flying."

She took over her set of controls, felt out the plane's response to bar and stick, tore through a little bank of woolpack, and sailed out into the bright sun again on even keel.

When he saw she could handle the ship safely, Noel leaned back and lit a cigarette, glad to be relieved of the piloting. His shoulder and arm ached, where the Goulet *métis* had struck him with the spiked scantling; and two straight nights without sleep had fagged him badly.

Through half-closed eyes he studied the delicate profile of Harla's lips and nose and throat. A trickle of slipstream, sifting through the horizon pane, was fluttering the nosegay of fire-flowers at her breast. Her hand on the leather-wrapped stick looked ridiculously small to be guiding a plane through the air at a hundred and forty an hour.

From stray bits of information last night at the dance, he knew almost exactly her motive for this Manitou trip. She and Jimmy had been very near to each other. Born and reared in northern Ontario, they had been orphaned in their teens, had run their father's trading post for a time, had gone away to school together, had stuck together till Jimmy tired of ablative absolutes and blew west.

Without question, Jimmy had written *her* about his secret; and when those unknowns began hounding him, he probably had written her about that, too. In alarm for him she had packed up instantly and started for the sub-Arctic. Those Dinokuis were merely a side issue; her main reason was this danger to her brother. Likely she was intending to make Jimmy drop his venture and get out of the North before he got killed.

By a matter of days she had come too late. Their very trails had crossed, somewhere in Saskatchewan or Manitoba, and neither had known of it. While she had been hurrying west to Edmonton and into the North, Jimmy had been flying east to Winnipeg and his anonymous grave.

With something of a jolt it came home to Noel that this girl sitting beside him had no relative on earth now and no understanding friend except his own self. In this whole huge country not one person, not even Harla herself, knew her situation or the dangers hovering over her or the tragedy that she was running headlong into. He alone knew. He alone could guard and protect her.

Last evening, over that soda in the drug store, fate or hapchance or destiny had given this girl into his hands, as a sacred trust. Whatever happened between them in the days ahead, she was his to shield, and her claim on him came first. For Jimmy he could do nothing now except to exact revenge. But he could shield Harla and see that she came out of this alive. That he must do. The claim of the living was stronger than the claim of the dead ....

Two hundred miles deep in the Grand Marais, he took over the controls again. A few minutes later, above a big lake with a rocky islet in the deep-water center, he glanced down idly and watched the Diomede's shadow sweeping up across the flag beds along the west shore.

As he gazed at the shadow and the innumerable muskrat houses, his eyes suddenly picked up, on those flag beds far below, a sight that took him like a club-blow.

Down yonder, trailing the shadow of his Diomede, came a *second shadow*, sweeping up across those flags, drawing nearer, closing.

He whirled around, glanced through the left window, glanced back.

Out across the void a large gray monoplane, less than three hundred yards away, was pouncing upon the Diomede at full-gunned roar.

In that moment of his staring at the gray plane he realized, in flashes quicker than thought, that sometime during the four hours past, somewhere back in the Athabasca country, his enemies had sighted the Diomede in spite of all his precautions. They had swung in behind, followed at a safe distance, and let him fly on and on into this wild Slave country where no human ever came. Now they were striking at him, to knock his little ship out of the air and send it plummeting downward into that slimy-green ooze where it would be lost till the end of time.

Before he could push the stick forward and dive, the gray craft opened on the little plane with a withering blast. Above the engine noise came a sinister *ratt-tatt-tt-tt*. From a cowl trap in that gray ship's window leaped reddish spurts of fire; and the white smoking lines of tracer bullets came streaking across, guiding the aim of that enemy gunner.

A tattoo of sharp impacts struck the Diomede, beating against the wings and fuselage like violent hailstones. The ship lurched and wobbled crazily. In the window beside Noel the glass shattered to bits, and the cold slipstream swirled in like a deluge of icy water. Across the instrument board a row of neatly patterned little holes suddenly appeared, as though by magic, smashing compass and aneroid, scattering glass and splinters and bits of metal all over the cabin.

To dodge the gray annihilation swooping upon him and Harla, Noel knocked the throttle up to full revv, shoved the stick forward, and went whistling downward in a giddy spiral dive.

His sudden maneuver shook the enemy craft. With its white tracers futilely trying to tilt down and catch him again, it roared over him, vanished like an evil apparition into a bank of woolpack; and for a few seconds it was lost to sight.

At four thousand feet Noel came out of the long dive, managed to steady the careening plane, and leveled it off. His first numbing shock had passed; he was thinking, trying to fight off the death overhead. If that plane closed in again and one of those smoking tracers hit a gas tank, the Diomede would be a mass of flames in a handful of seconds.

"Noel! What happened?" The sudden appearance of the gray ship and the crashing suddenness of that machine-gun burst had stunned her. "Those men in that plane—were they trying to *kill us?*"

"Yes!" he jerked out, tight-lipped. A fury had seized him, was shaking him to his depths. Those wanton killers, turning a machine gun on a girl, an innocent girl, in order to get him—it was as brutal and cold-hearted as that mocking laugh when they had murdered her brother.

He kicked the Diomede around in a hairpin bank and headed west for the Slave River, for Fort James or Northumbria or any post he could make. With only a light rifle and a pocket automatic, he and Harla stood no chance against that withering machine gun. Their lives were a question of outdistancing that enemy plane to a post and human help.

Forty miles to the Slave, a hundred miles to Fort James—the speedy Diomede might make it.

"But—but who are those men?" Harla cried.

Noel reached for the gas-tank lever. "Some enemies of mine!" He yanked at the lever, meaning to dump both wing tanks and lighten the little Diomede. The emergency tank would get him to Fort James. But the lever cable had been shot in two; the lever hung limp and useless; he was unable to dump the tanks.

As he shielded his eyes from the slipstream and looked westward for a glimpse of the Slave, the motor started coughing, spluttering; the revv needle began falling; the air speed dropped.

"Look up, see where that plane is!" he ordered Harla, fighting frantically with throttle and hand pump to keep the engine from going out. "D'you see those men anywhere?"

Harla pressed her face against the window and looked upward. "They're out of that cloud; they're almost straight overhead; they're slanting down in front of us. You'd better swing! They're coming fast, they're going to shoot at us again."

Noel kicked the sluggish Diomede around to dodge this second thrust.

With sinking heart he realized that the engine had been disabled and was going to konk, in spite of anything he could do. One of those bullets had punctured the feed line or hit some vital spot in the ignition. The motor was choking, the revv was falling away to nothing; the controls were dangerously limp and soggy. In a minute more he would have no engine at all.

The Slave was out. A post and human help—that was out. He dared not even try to glide a few miles toward the Slave. That gray plane would swim up alongside, run another burst at point-blank range, either kill him and Harla outright or turn the stricken little Diomede into a holocaust of flames. He had to get out of the air, get down, get himself and Harla out of the ship, and get shelter from that deadly gun—if he could.

With a glance at the lake below, he dived again, aiming at the rocky islet in the lake center. The islet was hardly larger than a garden plot, but it was solid ground, not quivering bog. Among its gray-lichened boulders he and Harla might find some sort of cover.

The laboring motor konked and died, but at the steep slant the Diomede was picking up speed, the controls were firming and tightening. In a strange silence, a silence that throbbed loudly after long hours of constant engine roar, the plane went swishing down toward the rocky islet.

"Take a look—that other ship—where is it now?" he demanded of Harla.

She glanced back. Though she had recovered a little from the paralyzing shock of the attack, she was still breathless and bewildered.

"You threw them off; they're more than a mile away—over at the west side of this lake. But they're banking, swinging and dropping... Now they're heading for us. Noel! Who are they? Why are they trying——?"

"Don't ask questions *now!* Look down ahead. See that island? We've got to whip ashore there. Got to get into that rock jumble. I'll plow into the shallows. In close. If we're slow about it, that machine gun will cut us down. Grab your rifle from the rack. Get our outfits ready. We've got to have them and your gun."

Harla pulled down her rifle, but the outfits had tumbled back behind the rear seat and were wedged tight; and in the careening plane she managed to free only Noel's blanket roll.

Fish-tailing to kill his speed, Noel dropped for the water, at a dangerous angle. With a splash and terrific impact the Diomede hit the surface a hundred yards from the islet, bounced up again, smacked the water a second time, bumped on into the shallows till the pontoons scraped the muck and dug in and grounded solidly—with a jolt that threw Noel and Harla against the instrument board.

Noel tried to fling open his cabin door, but it was jammed. Smashing at it with the butt of the rifle, he broke it open, leaped out upon the left float and helped Harla down.

He intended to spring back into the cabin and grab their outfits and that creel of food. Without food or any means of protection against the torturing insect hordes, their chances of keeping alive in this appalling muskeg country were next to nothing, even if they did find temporary refuge in the rocks yonder and were able to fight off these enemies. And he had to get those things now or he never would. That gray plane would land, taxi in to easy range, set the Diomede afire and destroy the little ship.

But he had no chance to get back into the cabin and gather up their outfits.

The enemy plane, less than a thousand yards away, was hurtling straight at them.

"Come on! Hurry it!" he cried at Harla, who was waiting on his leadership. He reached inside the cabin and grabbed his blanket roll—the first thing to hand—and seized Harla's arm. "Those two big rocks there by the little juniper—we'll get down between them. If that gun catches us in the open, we're done for."

They jumped into the knee-deep water and splashed ashore, with Noel carrying the blanket roll and rifle. The muck slowed them down.

As they raced across the slippery landwash, the gray plane thundered into range, and that ominous *ratt-tatt-tt-tt-tt* opened on them again.

Noel put himself between Harla and the gun, and held the blanket roll so that it shielded her head and shoulders.

Bullets *splaated* into the mud around them, hissed into the water, caromed off the lichened rocks and ricocheted out through the air. But the low trajectory and the speed of the plane destroyed the gunner's concentration; and the new belt he was using had no tracers to help him pick up his quarry.

They reached the juniper untouched.

As they scrambled in between the two granite boulders, the gray plane roared overhead, so low that they felt the blast of its slipstream.

CHAPTER SEVEN

I T seemed to Harla that the long dreadful day would never end. Her wristwatch said ten o'clock at night, but a rim of the sun still showed above the northwest horizon, and twilight had just started to settle over the marshy lake.

Beside her, in the little niche where they had been besieged for fifteen hours, Noel was lying asleep, half curled around the tiny smudge which they had built to fight off the mosquitoes and swarming *brûlés*.

How anybody could calmly lie down and go to sleep in a plight like theirs—hungry, wet, muddy; no food, no boat, no outfit; imprisoned on this islet; stranded in this wilderness of bog and lonely waters—it was more than she could understand. But he had done it. "Guess I'd better catch a bit of rest, Harla, so I'll be feeling fit for our break-away tonight," he had said to her, five hours ago. "Call me at ten, won't you?" As coolly and casually as that!

She wished that she had a little of his *sang-froid*. She was tired, thirsty, hungry; the smoke stung her eyes; her face and hands were badly bitten despite the smudge; and her spirits were at a low ebb generally.

In the shallows fifty yards away lay all that was left of the brave little Diomede—its gaunt fire-blackened skeleton of steel and lattice iron. On the open water seven hundred yards beyond, the big gray plane rode triumphantly at anchor, with its machine gun trained on the islet, and two canvas canoes bobbing alongside the floats.

So far as she could see, that plane did not carry a single identification letter or symbol. Gray and mysterious, it seemed like an anonymous gray death, ranging these wild lands. And those six men in it, wearing heavy leather clothes and masked with mosquito veils, seemed more like apparitions of evil than men of flesh and blood.

Those six, yonder, plainly had no intention of closing in and making a head-on attack. Possibly they had witnessed that shooting contest at McMurray and knew she could do things with a rifle. They were calmly waiting, confident that another day of hunger, thirst and insect torture would drive their two victims to the open, where that big-barreled Vickers would have its chance at them.

In her despairing mood, her and Noel's plan to break out of this siege looked like a sure-fire failure, certain to end in their getting shot or drowned.

Even if they did get away from these men, the Slave River was forty miles distant. Forty *muskeg* miles. She knew muskeg and she knew "flies." That river was almost as forlorn a goal as the mountains of the moon.

The smudge had burned low; the mosquitoes and flies were beginning to sift into the niche. She leaned forward and brushed a vicious *brûlé* from Noel's temple and spread her kerchief on his face. A "strike-first," big as a hornet, came whining in and hit her cheek and drew blood where it struck.

That little twinge of pain was like the last straw with her, and she leaned her head against the hard granite rock and cried. Stranded, hopelessly stranded, eight hundred miles from Manitou, just when she needed so desperately to be there and help Jimmy—or find him—or find out what had happened to him... Why hadn't he answered the urgent wireless she sent him from Ottawa? Or her second wireless, from Edmonton? Or the third, from McMurray? Jimmy had never got those messages. Why hadn't he? Where was he? Those enemies whom he had mentioned in his last letter—had they finally trapped him and—— But she pushed *that* thought away from her, violently.

When she calmed herself and looked out again, in the purple twilight of ten-thirty, four of those men were clambering out of the gray plane, with rifles and paddles, and getting into the canoes, two men to each.

As the canoes pushed away from the ship, she reached for her rifle, thinking that they were going to skirl in and attack, in the failing light. But instead of coming any nearer, they started to make a wide circle around the islet, one canoe going east and the other going west; and with a gasp of dismay she realized that they intended to patrol the island, during the brief half-dark, and see that their prisoners did not escape.

"Cowards!" she flung at them. "Six of you, with a machine gun, and you're too yellow to face one man and a girl!"

A few minutes later Noel stirred and sat up. "Hello. How's everything been on the western front?" Through the "door" of their boulder niche he caught a glimpse of the patrolling canoes. The sight of them did not seem to daunt him the slightest. "Hmmph! All they'll get out of that is exercise and mosquito bites. We're going to leave this place, girl."

His assurance, as firm and hard as the granite rock that she leaned against, lifted Harla a little from her despair. Danger, to this companion of hers, seemed part of the day's work. The shadow of death seemed an old acquaintance of his.

Noel crept outside cautiously for juniper bark and lichen, came back, replenished their smudge.

As a piece of bark flared into tiny flame, lighting up the lean jaw and gray unfathomable eyes of her companion, Harla found herself, for the hundredth time that day, trying to pierce the hard silence that clothed him. Who was he? No knock-about prospector, as he purported to be. Versatile and smooth, he played the rôle not badly, but he simply was not of the tribe. Essentially he was a city person.

A strange background it must have taken to produce so case-hardened a man—calmly sleeping when a machine gun was trained upon him. He must have run a gamut of experiences that ordinary people never even dreamed about. He had lived dangerously, on some strange frontier of life. There *were* frontiers in the cities. Dark and little-known frontiers. Wild lands in the hearts of men. And there this companion of hers had lived.

From his face her eyes went to the blackened skeleton of the Diomede, yonder; and an unbearable harassment welled up in her. She would never know, now, whether that ship had been Jimmy's own. Unless this man told her. And he would not speak.

"Noel!"—her anxiety and suspicions came breaking out. All day she had fought to keep her thoughts to herself; but she could no longer fight them back.

"What, Harla?" He leaned forward, solicitous toward her; and the little flame lit up his features clearly. "What's the trouble, girl?"

"You!" she flashed at him. "Why don't you try telling me the truth about yourself and these men? I've got a right to know. I'm into this fix as deep as you are."

"The truth?" he echoed, frowning as though perplexed. His face was a picture of bewilderment. "I don't get you."

"You do, you do get me! You lied to me about yourself. A prospector, you? You're a million miles from being one. And this feud between yourself and these men—don't tell me again that it's 'just a little bad blood over a claims dispute.' It's a war, a vicious and brutal war; and you're party to it!"

She paused for breath, then stormed on: "You haven't told me one truthful word about yourself. Won't your business in this country bear daylight? Are you afraid for your real name to be known? That's what I think. You wouldn't be hiding your name and business if you didn't have to! I've been trying to believe well of you, but I can't. You may have brains and class and all that, but I'd rather associate with an *honest* person, like Strap."

He winced at that. It surprised Harla that her words could cut him so deeply, when he was proof against nearly everything else. As he stirred uneasily under the lash of her charges, she was contrite for her outbreak. Into her mind came the memory of how Noel had shielded her with his own body that morning as they raced across the land-wash through the spray of bullets, and of how he dashed outside that afternoon and brought her a drink of water at risk of death from that machine gun.

To her amazement Noel did not say a word in his own defense. After a few moments he said quietly: "I'm sorry you think I'm a liar and worse, Harla. But let it go. For the present at least, let's try to be friends. We're in the same boat, we're into some bad white water; and we've got to go down through it together. Let's save our lives, if we can, and then"—he forced a smile—"then we can quarrel."

It was on her lips to demand point-blank: "That Diomede *was* my brother's, and how did you get it?" But she kept silent, not mortally sure about the plane. And wariness cautioned her not to throw down all her cards. Though she could not quite believe it, there was a chance that this stony-silent companion of hers might be one of Jimmy's enemies. Might even be their superbly capable leader, whom Jimmy had mentioned.

That Diomede—there was the heart of the question. If the ship really had been her brother's, then this man was one of those enemies. He had to be. Jimmy had had no friend, no partner.

As she looked at Noel, across the little flame, knowing positively that he had lied to her about himself and his feud with these men, she felt all but certain that he was lying about the plane, too. When she thought about the fears in Jimmy's last letter and about his ominous silence since then, a shudder went through her at the memory of how she had danced last night with this man ....

The sun finally inched out of sight but its beautiful orange afterglow lingered. The broken clouds overhead were streaked with weird gigantic shadows cast by peaks of the Rocky Mountains two hundred miles away. In the flag beds at the west side of the lake Harla heard the familiar slap of beaver and muskrat. Night-feeding ducks started up their sociable gabbling. Through the gathering dusk came the whir of bullet-swift curlew wings, the laugh of a red-throated loon, the *zoom* of bullbats tilting and banking.

She turned her wristwatch to the tiny glow. On this breakaway she was tacitly taking the lead, because of her bush-loping experience.

"Eleven o'clock; we ought to be leaving," she said to Noel, trying hard to be matter-of-fact with him. As he had said, they were in the same boat, the same desperate plight; and she had to accept partnership with him whether she liked it or not. "Before we go we'll fix a smudge that will last several hours. As long as those men see a good smudge going, they'll think we're still here."

Noel slipped outside for reeds and bark and wet moss. After mixing the dry stuff with the damp sphagnum, Harla arranged the material in a little long ridge and lighted one end of it.

Reluctantly they abandoned Harla's rifle. On the dark gantlet ahead it would be too heavy a drag. They dared take nothing but two wire-weaves from the blanket roll.

Glad to leave their cramped hot prison, they crept out of the rock nest and down to the last small boulder on the west landwash.

The afterglow had faded from the high clouds, and the major stars were out. The gray plane was invisible, and the canoe patrolling that west side was only a dim mottle on the water.

While Harla unlaced her boots and slipped off her outer clothes, she listened to the slapping of the nearest muskrats and beavers, and fixed the direction in mind—straight toward red Mars above the western horizon.

They wrapped their boots and clothes and Noel's automatic in the blankets; made a compact little bundle, spindle-shaped so that it would push through the water easily; and laced it tightly with a boot-cord.

Bent low, they slipped across the muddy landwash into the shallows. Keeping watch on that sinister mottle ahead, they waded out, yard by cautious yard, to chin-deep water. There they stopped to reconnoiter.

The patrolling canoe, making a semi-circular beat around that west side, was swinging back toward them. They watched it draw nearer. A scant hundred yards away it halted, the men lit cigarettes, drifted a minute to rest, then went on.

"They'll be ten minutes getting back, in that clumsy canvas tub," Harla whispered, as the canoe grew dimmer. "By then we'll easily be across that patrol line and out of sight beyond. Let's go."

They started swimming—across the deep water toward the western shore.

Before they had gone two rods Harla saw that Noel was even a poorer swimmer than he had let her know, when they planned this break-away. He was slow, he had no stroke better than a dog-paddle, and his splashes were dangerously loud.

She stopped and allowed him to draw up even.

"Let me take the bundle," she bade. And when he protested, she took it from his unwilling hand. "We've got to get across that patrol line in a hurry. Lie flatter in the water and don't fight so hard."

By a valiant struggle he succeeded in keeping up with her till they were across the canoe beat. Fifty yards beyond it, Harla glanced back and spotted that sinister mottle again, so close that she could see the two men and the moon-glint on their rifles.

"Sh-hh-hh," she warned. "Keep down to your nose. We'll tread water till they get past. Don't break surface. They might see the gleam."

As she waited through that endless minute, she realized that Noel could never possibly make it to the first muskrat colony.

Already, with less than a fourth of their distance behind them, he was tired out and barely able to keep afloat.

"All clear," she whispered finally, as that fearsome mottle slowly faded out of sight. "We're through the danger zone. A bit more swimming, and we'll be free. Take it easy. It's only a little distance to where we can wade."

Keeping watch on Noel, she turned over and began a tireless back crawl, conserving her strength for the hard pull that was looming up.

For a little while, another hundred yards, Noel managed to battle on through the dark waters. But then he began floundering and gasping for breath.

She glided alongside. "Put your hand on me. I'll help you."

"I—I won't. It'd drag you down."

"Nonsense. Swimming comes natural to me, just as it comes unnatural to you. Do as I tell you, unless you insist on drowning in your manly pride."

She started swimming again, pushing the bundle and half towing Noel. It was a bad drag; the bundle was waterlogged, her clothes were a bother, and that hand on her shoulder was heavier than she had reckoned on. Time after time a little quiver of panic darted through her, and she was tempted to throw all her strength into a reckless dash for those shallows.

But she fought the impulse down. With even rhythmic strokes she forged steadily on and on, glancing now and then at her guide star, red Mars.

Sooner than she had expected, from her survey of the lake that afternoon, she came into shallows, and her feet touched mucky bottom.

"Sorry I was such a wash-out," Noel said, as they stopped for a minute. "I really thought I could make that swim. I won't say 'Thank you' for saving my life out there, Harla. That would sound too common and cheap for what I feel."

Harla made no reply. Glancing back, she saw the red pin-point of their smudge, still burning, still lulling the suspicion of their enemies; but of the plane and those canoes she saw nothing, heard nothing. The lake was dark and asleep.

She led the way to the first muskrat house, and they crawled out upon the matted reeds.

As Harla put on her clothes she was thinking not so much that they had slipped past those pitiless rifles and broken out of the siege as that she had squared accounts with this gray-eyed companion of hers. For his saving her when that gray plane struck, for that drink of water and his other kindnesses, she had paid him back in full; and now she could feel toward him as she liked, without twinge of conscience.

They were two hours swimming and wading across the quivery bog to the west shore of the lake. There, in the gray dawn, they struck drier ground.

Hungry, mud-plastered and bitten raw by the flies, they had to halt.

That one mile of battle against the muskeg had entirely wiped out Harla's elation over their escape. One mile had exhausted them, and they had *forty* ahead. Many a seasoned and well-equipped "northern man," venturing along the mere fringe of this Grand Marais, had perished; and she and Noel were stranded in the very heart of it, without food or rifle or outfit. And in a few hours that plane would be hunting for them, beating over this lake shore.

She had hopes of making a raft, but if they did they would have more than a hundred miles to go, in those tortuous dead-water channels. A hundred miles of poling through mud and flags. A week of starvation and flies and exposure.

With Noel's knife they hacked small squares from a blanket and made clumsy mittens to protect their hands and wrists. From larger squares they fashioned themselves two parka-like hoods, with slits for mouth and eyes. The hoods were crazy-looking but effective in a rough way.

From the west shore the ground sloped gently up to a small ridge a quarter-mile distant. Tufted with squat balsam and streaked with the gray of windfall, the crest was less than twenty feet above lake level, but in that flat desolation it loomed against the sky with all the impressiveness of a sizable mountain range.

No longer so cruelly punished by the flies, she led the way through the tangled buckbrush to the top of the elevation, and they looked westward.

The Slave, their goal, was out of sight below the horizon. To the limit of vision in every direction stretched a wild expanse of slimy-green prairions, lakes and crisscross sloughs and stagnant channels without flow—the dreaded "Dead Waters" of the voyageurs. The flag swamps, huge and impenetrable, swarming with waterfowl and water animals, were restless with the thrash and wallow of life. On the larger lakes floated acres of molting ducks and geese, naked, helpless, keeping to deep water for safety against the mink and otter of the flags.

On the lake behind, the gray plane still rode at anchor; the two canoes had stopped patrolling and come in; the smudge was still sending up a thin wisp of smoke.

At first glance the confusion of waters to the west seemed to Harla like an utter chaos, without order or plan; but as she studied the region she discerned a certain rough method in its layout. Starting with a little plover pond just down slope, a chain of lakes of increasing size led westward, connected by narrow blue-water channels. Those channels looked to her like segments of an old sunken river. Likely that lake chain constituted a drainage system, of a sort, to the Slave.

"Even if it isn't," she told Noel, "that chain leads west, our direction. But what looks good to me is the blue water. That means *deep* water; and that means no portaging. With us a portage would be a disaster."

Listening for the gray plane, they hunted along the ridge, selected a dozen small windfall logs and poles, toted them down to the pond edge, and made a little six-by-ten raft, fastening the timbers together with willow withes in lieu of spikes or *babische*.

The raft was a clumsy unsubstantial thing, and Harla eyed it with misgiving. A bit of wind on one of those broad lakes would tear it to pieces.

Not daring to embark while the gray plane was around, she and Noel pushed the raft back into a flag bed, covered it over with brush, and returned to the higher ground.

So hungry that they had been chewing on lichen as they worked, they made a determined hunt along the slope for something to eat. In a juniper thicket they found a clump of bearberries and picked a handful each. The sour red fruit only made them hungrier. Along a gray-rock ledge they discovered a patch of bracken, and grubbed out a few of the tasteless watery bulbs.

That was all the food on the whole ridge; and the ridge was the only dry land within sight.

"Just take a look out across there," Noel bade, gesturing at the lakes, at the floating shoals of fat plump ducks and geese. "Thousands of 'em! Hundreds of thousands of 'em! And they're all ready to cook—they haven't even got feathers on 'em! And not a one can we get! But we will get one! Tonight I'll wade out into one of those flocks, with my automatic; and I'll get us a big fat goose—*apiece!*"

Toward mid-morning, when they were combing along the pond edge in hopes of clubbing a stray waterfowl or finding a belated brant nest, they heard the motor of the gray plane. Knowing that their escape had been discovered, they hurried up to the ridgeline and hid themselves under a squat balsam, to watch.

When its engine was warm the plane pulled anchor, skimmed across the water, jumped into the air, circled once above the rocky islet and came winging over toward that west shore.

Harla expected the ship to land, put off men and make a thorough search. To her astonishment the plane made only a brief perfunctory hunt—merely a quick survey to see that they were nowhere in bold sight. After sweeping up along that west shore once, it climbed high in a steep spiral and lined away into the northwest.

As the plane disappeared and its distant drone died to nothing, she looked at Noel; and by the gloom on his face she knew that he too understood this strange move. That ship was not making a trip for gas. It had gone for good, leaving them there in the heart of the Grand Marais. Those men had made no hunt for the simple reason that they considered a hunt useless work, useless risk of accident. They considered that two people, stranded in that watery desolation, were quite as good as dead.

"I—I'd rather they'd have—have hunted for us," she sobbed, breaking down and crying. She was weak from hunger and exhaustion; that muskeg wilderness appalled her; but the worst blow of all was the utter confidence of these men, these unknown of the North, that she and Noel could never get out alive.

"Don't, partner," Noel soothed. "Don't cry or give up. We're not licked. We'll show that outfit whether we're dead or not." He put his arm around her and patted her encouragingly; and she felt his lips touch her hair. "You're too brave a girl to give up a fight. We'll get through, honey. We've got a raft, and we'll get a goose; and in a week from now we'll be poling out upon the Slave."

Trying hard to catch his faith and his grimly defiant mood, she let him lead her down to the pond edge.

There they pulled their raft from the bulrushes, clambered upon it, took up their poles, and started on their "voyage" westward to the master stream.

On the broad muddy Slave, a trapper, leaning against the bow rail of the *Midnight Sun,* suddenly straightened up and peered across at the far eastern shore of the river.

"Hey!" he cried, seizing a near-by trader by the arm. "Lookit, Seth! What the dickens is that thing, over yon?"

The trader looked, blinked his eyes, looked again. "Why, it appears like a raft! A raft and a coupla people! And they're waving something. Get that pair of glasses from the wheelhouse!"

The trapper ran for the binoculars, came back, focused them on the distant object.

His yell went up and down the length of the *Midnight Sun.*

"Holy hell! It's a girl and a man! They're waving at *us!* It's that DeLong girl and that Lanier fellow. It's them two that got lost and the whole country's been hunting for. Get a boat and fetch 'em in!"

CHAPTER EIGHT

O N THE *Midnight Sun,* Noel found the friendly crowd of Three Rivers people, home bound for Northumbria, Manitou and the Arctic posts on beyond, a potential gold mine of information to him.

As soon as he and Harla were squared around and he had answered the deluge of questions about his "plane mishap" in the Grand Marais, he went to work on his fellow travelers, digging for clues to this pack and to Jimmy's baffling secret.

Through the long lazy days and brief nights, as the *Midnight Sun* bore him on toward Manitou, he loafed against the rail and talked with prospectors who had wandered the lone dim rivers of the Arctic Rockies and the musk-ox prairies of the Great Barrens. In the smoking room he played endless pinochle with three veteran Mounted non-coms, returning to duty at isolated posts. He sat around on the deck cargo and hobnobbed with Mackenzie trappers who had taken their peltry tucks to the Edmonton auction and squandered a whole winter's harsh toil on a week of bright lights. He made friends with some Yellowknife half-breeds from Manitou district, and quizzed a factor and Anglican missionary from Manitou itself.

For all his expert digging, he turned up no clue whatever to those enemies. They seemed clothed with a dark impenetrable silence. No person had ever glimpsed or even heard of that gray ghostly plane. The very existence of any outlaw pack in this North was utterly unsuspected.

"Hmmph! They're operating behind some respectable front, just like myself," he reflected. A part of them at least were northern men, intimately acquainted with this country. Back in the savage hinterland, away from the main Three Rivers route, they had secret camps and gas caches. There they were keeping this machine-gunned ship religiously out of sight; and from those hidden bases they had carried on their cruelly one-sided war against Harla's brother.

Almost everybody aboard, he found, had known and liked Jimmy "Chantrell"; and he speedily acquired a broad picture of the youngster's two years in the North. Without partner or confidant, Jimmy had lived alone in a cabin at Manitou. Using pontoons in summer and skis in winter, he was absent on almost continual prospecting trips. Sometimes he was gone only a few hours, sometimes a whole month. Though he never brought back any ore specimens or filed any claim papers, he seemed intensely absorbed in his work.

Jimmy's odd way of life had naturally aroused curiosity; and many and wild were the guesses about him. Jimmy was a "wanted man" who had fled to the oblivion of the North. Jimmy had struck a gold-placer prize and was working it on the quiet. Jimmy was doing secret exploration for some big mining company. Jimmy was a rich man's son, taking the wilderness cure. Jimmy was this, that and the other.

To all these guesses Noel listened patiently, skeptically, winnowing grains of fact from bushels of chaff.

Among the people aboard was a girl called Alice Wentworth, returning from a summer vacation at Calgary. The government schoolmistress at Manitou for the last two years, she lived in a cabin just a few rods from Jimmy's. When Noel heard about this and heard also that she and Jimmy had been rather close associates, he sorted her out for special attention, made friends with her, and deftly pumped the girl.

To his utter amazement Alice knew nothing at all about Jimmy's venture. For two whole years she had been the youngster's closest friend, had seen his daily personal life; and yet she was completely in the dark.

In exasperation he was tempted to turn to Harla, the one person aboard who did know Jimmy's secret. But she was the one person to whom he dared not go. She was suspicious of him already. To try any probing with her would be like touching a match to a powder barrel.

Besides, Harla would scarcely speak to him. At times during their fugitive days and nights in the Grand Marais she had been comradely; but those occasions had been rare and brief. Always something seemed to blow across her mind like a gust of freezing wind across the lake. Now, no longer forced to associate with him, she was keeping an aloof distance. In the purple owl-dusk of evening, in the roseate morning sun, she would pass him with a curt nod, her eyes cold and friendless.

As he looked back on that week in the Grand Marais, it seemed all a chaotic timeless blur, in which only his girl partner and the sweetness of her company stood out clearly. Their fiery ordeal of danger and terrific hardship had shown him that she was one of the few truly fine people whom he had ever known. Though he fought to blank her out of his emotions and drive ahead with his hunt, he could no more stop thinking about her and loving her than he could stop breathing.

Several times, when he felt particularly defeated and blue and lonely, he sought her out, on the steamer, and tried to win back the warm promising friendship of that evening at McMurray. It was hopeless. With her that friendship had died. In her eyes he was a suspicious character, a man wearing a mask because he dared not show his face. He could not blame her, under the circumstances; but her coldness hurt just the same—hurt him as few things in his life had done.

He was very much surprised, when he returned to his cabin one midnight, to find Harla waiting for him there. She was standing by the open port window, with the river breeze molding her dress about her, and the feeble electric light gleaming on the big silver buckle of her belt.

"Harla!" he greeted. The mere sight of her set his blood pounding. For a moment he thought that her visit was friendly; and a little rush of gladness swept away all his moodiness of that evening.

Harla's cold tones quickly disillusioned him. "I wirelessed my Ottawa bank yesterday for money, Mr. Lanier, and the reply came today. I'm here to pay you what I owe."

"Owe? Why, what do you owe me for?"

"For that gas at McMurray."

Noel was astonished. "Heavens, you don't owe me for that. We made no definite arrangement, and besides I didn't deliver my part—getting you to Manitou."

"The failure was not your fault; and I told Strap Barclay, positively, that I would pay for the gas. That's what I insist on doing."

Her proffer, more than the cold tones of it, was a cruel shock to Noel. She wanted to pay him this money as a kind of quittance. Wanted to free herself from the last vestige of debt or obligation to him.

As he met her gaze he was shaken with impulse to tell her, point-blank, then and there, that he was ex-Inspector Noel Irving, risking his life in a thankless hunt for the murderers of her brother. With a few words he could rip her suspicion to shreds and change the whole complexion of her opinion.

His good sense clamored at him to speak up now before his chance forever passed. His relationship with Harla was already damaged enough; and he had a premonition that it was heading toward a swift and complete disaster, unless he stopped that fatal drift by the one means in his power.

But those few words from him might cost Harla her life, and they would surely dynamite this hunt of his. When a girl's very life was at stake, it would be small of him, small and selfish, to let his own feelings enter in at all.

While he stood silent, looking at her, Harla counted out a number of bills and tendered them to him; and when he shook his head, she laid them on his berth.

Noel wanted to throw the bills through the window into the river; but cold reason told him to pocket his pride and take them. He was penniless. In the destruction of the Diomede he had lost everything but his automatic and the clothes he stood in. Unless he got funds somewhere, he would have to leave the *Midnight Sun* at Northumbria. The captain had so informed him, a few hours ago. This money would take him on to Manitou.

"All right," he said finally, with an effort, with a somewhat twisted smile. "You're very square, Harla. Thank you very much—and good night."

When she had gone he put the money in his pocket and sat down on the berth, looking with steady eyes at the relationship between Harla DeLong and himself. Until now he had believed that when his hunt was over and the curse of silence was lifted from him, he could easily enough set everything right. But he no longer believed so. That time was going to come too late. Relationships, except of trivial kind, did not go by sudden quirks and turns. It was the general drift that counted; and in this relationship the general drift was all against him. These early days and early stages of acquaintanceship were of profound importance. Harla's rational opinion of him might change but not her deep emotional attitude. As the twig is bent . . .

At Fort Northumbria, on the southern shore of Great Northumbria Lake, the *Midnight Sun* put in to discharge passengers and trading goods; and there a stranger came aboard.

Leaning against the bow rail and keeping an eye on the crowd, Noel saw the man come striding out upon the wharf, with an Indian carrying his rifle, dufflebag and other gear.

The man's sheer impressiveness, as he shouldered through the wharf crowd with a friendly "Hello, there!" or a "Howdy, partner!" to everybody, drew Noel's instant attention. Tall and superbly built, the stranger appeared to be about thirty-five, but he carried himself with the jaunty step of a much younger man. Boots muddy, face heavily bearded, shirt open at the neck, he seemed altogether careless of how he looked, with the careless nonchalance of a man who knew his own powers.

Catching sight of Harla, who was standing a little distance down the rail, he stopped and touched his hat gallantly.

"Hello, Miss DeLong, hello! Mighty good to see you again, alive and well. That was a happy moment for all of us when the flash came that you and Mr.—Lanier, isn't it?—had been picked up."

Harla merely nodded, coldly, without answering.

As the stranger strode on for the gangway, Noel walked down along the rail.

"Who's your handsome friend, Harla?"

"If you please, don't refer to him as a friend of mine."

"I'm sorry. I merely meant that he seems to know you."

"He was at McMurray. Two days before you came."

"Who is he?"

"His name is Flood, Raphael Flood. He's buying up claims in this country. At least, so he says."

"You don't believe that?"

"Not at all. It's pretty generally known what he really is doing. He's a railway consulting expert. The government brought him from South America. He's making a preliminary survey for this proposed railroad from Peace Landing up along the eastern flank of the Rockies."

To himself Noel smiled. At McMurray and on the steamer he had heard endless talk about this chimerical railway, this thousand-mile line over impossible muskeg and mountain. With these isolated northern people that line had been a cherished day-dream for years; and they fully believed it was coming. From his own inside contact with official Ottawa, he knew that the government had never remotely contemplated the fantastic project.

Flood, therefore was not in this country on any railroad business. Who was the man, then? And where had this empty rumor started?

In a few minutes, just long enough to have tossed his luggage into his cabin, Flood came walking up the fore deck. With the suspicion that here at last might be one of those enemies, if not the leader of that pack, Noel sized the man up as the latter approached. Dark-brown hair, hawk-sharp eyes, a bit of swagger about him and on his lips a faint perpetual smile of self-confidence, he was an unforgettable person, a man of high caliber and of great personal magnetism.

All the people of that fore deck turned and stared at him; and the gaze of the women especially—the *métise* girls, the traders' wives, Alice Wentworth—followed him with unconscious tribute. Noel remembered later, that of all those girls and women Harla DeLong was the sole one who had no use for Raphael Flood.

"I hope I'm not intruding," Flood said to Harla, as he confronted her and Noel.

Because she was compelled to, Harla introduced, "Mr. Flood, Mr. Lanier."

Flood reached out his hand, polite and friendly. "How d'you do, Lanier. It's a pleasure to meet a person who can whip the Grand Marais. Few men ever have done that."

In the man's tones, in his steady level eyes, Noel failed to detect the slightest flicker of enmity or the slightest knowledge that he, Flood, was face to face with ex-Inspector Noel Irving.

Except for a certain pique at finding Harla DeLong in the company of another man, Flood showed no animosity, no undue interest, no betraying sign whatever.

Surely, Noel thought, this person could not be the man who had shot up his Winnipeg apartment, built that McMurray deadfall for him and blasted him out of the air last week. Surely that man could never look him in the eyes like this, without betrayal.

With a little jolt of uneasiness he perceived that Flood's attraction to Harla was no casual matter. The man had come straight from his cabin as though drawn to her; and his eyes were roving over her face and hair and throat in a way which Noel, respecting Harla as he did, resented deeply.

Flood pointed down the west landwash, past a line of trapper tents and chained-up husky teams. "A band of Dog-ribs from the Thelon Barrens are in for their treaty money, Miss DeLong, and they're camped yonder in that granite dip. As an Indian expert you'd find them worth visiting. May I take you down there? This boat won't leave for a couple of hours."

"Mr. Lanier has asked me to go there," Harla evaded.

This was news to Noel; but he quick-wittedly backed her up. "We're waiting till the wharf clears a bit."

Flood was visibly disappointed, but he took her refusal with good grace. "Then I'll send you a 'breed interpreter for your visit," he suggested. "Since we'll be fellow passengers to Manitou, I'll see you later, Lanier. And you too, Miss DeLong, if I may."

With a polite nod he turned away and left them.

Harla looked at Noel. "Sorry I made you lie for me."

"Quite all right," Noel said. The little incident cheered him more than anything in days. It showed him that during their fugitive week together Harla had learned that she could trust him implicitly in this particular way in which she did not trust Flood an inch.

"You don't seem to like Flood very much," he probed. "If it's any of my business, why not?"

Harla hesitated a moment. Then: "To be plain about it, I don't like men who're on the prowl. Flood's that. He's eternally that. I saw enough of him at McMurray to know." Her eyes flashed anger, as though she was recalling some incident at the steel-end hamlet. "It makes me furious for him to have me on his list of candidates, along with these *metises* and others."

She pointed at a large yellow Albatross anchored in the little bay. "That's his ship. Why isn't he flying to Manitou instead of going by slow boat? I'll tell you why—and I don't care if it does sound presumptuous of me. He thinks that he can put me in a hole by coming aboard here; that I can't avoid associating with him, on a little steamer like this. Well, I'll show him! I'm going to read him a riot act."

"Don't make an enemy of him if you can help it," Noel advised. Regardless of who Flood might be, it was unwise and possibly downright dangerous for a girl in Harla's situation, sub-stantially alone in this lonely elemental country, to antagonize a man of Flood's aggression. Flood was plainly infatuated with her, and infatuations took strange twists.

As he chatted with Harla, thankful for this little flicker of friendliness from her, he reflected: "Flood can't possibly be the leader of that pack. They deliberately tried to kill Harla, along with myself; and Flood would never have ordered that. He's too much taken with her."

On second thought he saw that those men might have acted on their own initiative. At the time of that attack Flood had been in the far North, at Manitou or Northumbria. Unable to consult him, his men might have used their own judgment, followed the Diomede and shot it down.

In a minute or two Flood's half-breed interpreter came up along the rail. A strapping young French-Chipewayan, color-fully dressed in beaded leather clothes, quilled moccasins and rainbow belt, he was a likable young *métis*, touched with the all picturesqueness of the old voyageur.

"How do, Mees, how do, frien'," he greeted them. *"Moi,* I'm Paul LaSalle d'Orleans; and don' you call me 'Sally,' lak some of dese pipple do. Flood ask me to go wit' you to dose Dog-reebs and do de back-and-fort' talk. Okay. *Allons."*

"You don't have to go, Paul," Harla said, refusing this favor from Flood. "I speak enough Tenneh to make out."

"You, Mees? *Sacrebleu!* I t'ought you was plenty cheechako. But okay—I don' lak dem raw-fish eaters nohow."

As Noel took Harla down to the gangway, he glanced across the aft deck and saw Flood, beside the anchor windlass, chatting with two *métise* girls from Fort James. The girls were a-flutter at his attention to them; and a dozen or more people had drawn near, listening, hunching closer, eager for a word or a glance from the man who was mapping a route for that thousand-mile railroad.

It suddenly occurred to Noel that this railroad rumor, this crazy gossip which made Flood a person of towering impor-tance to these guileless northern people, had been started by Flood himself. No one else would have any reason to start such a rumor. But Flood had plenty reason. It not only gave him this whole Three Rivers country as a stage for his prowling, but threw a perfect smokescreen over the man's real business in the North. Even Harla had been taken in by that rumor.

As Harla and he made their way ashore, the belief was run-ning strong in him that here at last, in Flood, in the person of their leader, that pack of unknowns had begun to emerge from the shadows.

CHAPTER NINE

ALONE on the bow deck, as the steamer yawed in to the pier, Noel gazed through the midnight dusk at tiny Manitou post, at the scatter of dim buildings and twinkling candlelights; and in a tight-lipped mood he wondered what unguessable avalanche was going to pile down upon him at this wilderness-buried *vedette*.

The avalanche would come, all right, and swiftly. This place was rendezvous for that pack, and they simply dared not let him live. Scared of him, of his relentless stalking, they would try to put him out of the picture, and that within a matter of hours.

The only question in his mind was the form which this avalanche would take. That was what daunted him—the nerve-racking uncertainty of what to expect from those men.

To the east, across the six-mile-broad Mackenzie, lay a rugged land of granite swells and poppy meadows—the threshold of the vast Arctic tundra. To the west, only an hour's walk back of the post, the foothills of the mighty Rockies began rising up; and by the lingering afterglow of the sun, hidden just below the northern horizon for this half hour at midnight, he could see beyond those foothills, a sweep of massive ice-crowned ranges towering darkly against the night sky.

In the midst of all that immensity of mountains and tundra and waters, the post itself, sprawled against a hillock that sloped from the river, seemed exactly what Strap Barclay had called it—a little fly-speck of a place.

Dimly, as the steamer yawed closer, Noel distinguished the H-B store, the gaunt frame mission, the white school-house where Alice Wentworth taught her dusky little flock, the wireless station and Mounted Police cabin, four clapboard dwellings, a few split-log *métis* shacks, and at the far woods edge a dozen leather tepees of visiting Indians.

Below the steamer wharf a plane rode at mooring—Flood's big cabined Albatross.

The smallness and brooding isolation of the post filled Noel with uneasy foreboding. At McMurray and on the *Midnight Sun* he had had around him many solid and dependable people, of good heart; but here he would be almost alone, cut off, uncertain about these folk, never knowing what man or men among them were his enemies.

The nearness of those wild ranges made him afraid, too, for Harla's safety. In the four days since Fort Northumbria he had seen much of Flood. Undisciplined, predatory, Flood was a man who took what he wanted, and he wanted Harla. On the steamer trip she had unwisely antagonized him, and her very inaccessibility had served to fan his infatuation ablaze.

Here, at Manitou, Harla would be living in the shadow of those mountains, of their fastnesses—in the shadow of a very real and fearsome danger.

For himself the last four days had been lonesome and bitterly disappointing. His hunt had slowed almost to a standstill. Except for some general insight into Flood's character, he had learned nothing about the man, nothing about his business on the Three Rivers. Whether or not Flood was the leader of that pack was still a raging question with him. For all he knew, Flood had no connection whatever with that shadowy outfit.

The ship was hushed; most of the passengers and crew were asleep below; but down near the gangway stood a little knot of dark figures, the people who were going ashore—Harla, Alice Wentworth, Flood and three others. A deckhand with lantern and freight trundler was moving their heavy luggage close to the plank head.

"*My* disembarking will be simple," Noel mused. "Matter of lighting a cigarette and strolling off."

As he gazed through the queer dark at Harla, sorting out her dim figure from all the others of that little group, he felt bitter and rebellious at his whole evil luck. One thin dime in his pocket, not one dependable friend in this huge North, no hope of help from the Mounted or the law, his very name in disgrace back in the city country—that was where he stood. And here was the crowning irony of it all, that Harla should so distrust and dislike him when he was fighting to avenge her brother.

He wished that he had not brought her north with him. In his growing pessimism there were times when he wished that he had never met or known her at all. What would happen between himself and her here at Manitou, only the veiled future knew; but he did know that it would take a cataclysm merely to undo the damage already done—and he had little faith in propitious cataclysms.

As the steamer scrunched against the wharf and was clewed fast, he walked down amidships. Harla was talking with Alice Wentworth, at whose cabin she had arranged to stay.

"May I help, may I see you and Alice to your cabin?" he offered.

"We'll get there nicely, thanks," Harla returned.

With his hand in his gun pocket Noel stepped down the plank, crossed the wharf, walked a rod or two up the grassy slope, slipped into the shadows of a fish scaffolding, and waited.

Presently Flood came past, alone. Then the H-B factor and the missionary. Then Alice and Harla.

Falling in behind the two girls, Noel silently trailed them on up toward their cabin, to make sure that Harla got safely there.

When they had entered Alice's place and he heard them fasten the door, he turned back and stole out along the slope to the little way-cabin which the northern pilots maintained and which Strap had invited him to use.

Inside, he dropped the door beam into place, groped in the dark for a pair of blankets, and pegged them tightly over the two small windows. Then, and only then, he lit the candle on the rough slab table.

Tired from days and nights of alert vigilance, he munched a few crackers and a bit of cheese from the cupboard; fixed up a rattle-bang contraption, with two pans and a string, so that no one could get into the cabin without waking him; and then, after snuffing the candle, he lay down on a bunk in the corner.

Despite his loneliness and the daunting memory of what those men had done to Jimmy, he felt a certain hard satisfaction—the only satisfaction he had—in knowing that step by step he was closing in upon his enemies, with the relentlessness of one not to be denied. From far-away Winnipeg, where he had started with only the vaguest of vague leads, he had followed their trail across the provinces to the threshold of the North, and on and on into the North itself, till now, here at this mountain-shadowed post, he had reached their rendezvous.

The rest was a matter of his keeping alive.

CHAPTER TEN

ARLY the next morning, so early that he felt positive Harla
would still be asleep, Noel started up the slope for Jimmy's
tenantless cabin, to make a thorough search of the place.

The morning was bright, fresh; the air had an invigorating tang; and the strange virile country around him, basking
under the northeast sun, was so beautiful that he hated to turn
his eyes and mind from it. In the tundra across the Mackenzie
the poppy meadows stretched in broad fields of yellow and
red, with the silver of lakes between. A blue translucent haze
half veiled the foothills; and beyond them the massive peaks,
with cap of ice and mantle of snow, were flashing cold brilliant
fires.

He wished that sometime the gods of his luck—stern gods
they had been, these thirteen years—might give him a season of
sunlit freedom in a land like this. But now he was bound to his
hunt. He had to live it, breathe it, and close his eyes to everything
else.

Around the H-B store and down at the wharf a number of
métis and swart Loucheaux were loafing in the sun. Young Paul
d'Orleans and a nondescript white man were pumping floats on
the Albatross and grooming the plane for flight. At the woods
edge beyond the mission stood Flood's large silk tent, fitted with
stove, mosquito door and other luxuries.

Except for looking Jimmy's cabin over, he intended to make
no investigation at all here at Manitou. His best strategy now was
not to expose himself by grubbing around for evidence but to sit

tight and wait. Those men were thoroughly scared, and they were going to make some move against him. If he gave them a good chance, they would trip themselves up.

Finding Jimmy's cabin unlocked, he stepped inside and closed the door.

As he glanced around, he was surprised at the expensive furnishings: a fine plushy rug, good draperies at the three large windows, a handsome heating stove, a radio, day bed, small mahogany desk.

Where had Jimmy got the money for all this and for that costly little Diomede? Without question, from this unknown venture of his. No wild-goose chase, that venture, but a solid lucrative fact.

Everything in the cabin lay exactly as Jimmy had left it, nearly a month ago, even to a half-eaten peppermint stick on the smoking-stand. On his flight south to the city country Jimmy had evidently pitched away in a great hurry. His bed was unmade, his muddied shirt and trousers were lying on the floor, the dishes of his last breakfast were still unwashed.

After opening a window to the fresh morning air, Noel began a swift search of the cabin.

He combed through the desk and bookcase; explored the couch and radio; scrutinized the walls for a hidden niche; stripped back the rug and examined the floor planking.

In the entire cabin there was not one clear hint to Jimmy's secret.

Disappointed, he lit a cigarette and leaned against the desk, groping for some explanation to this dark riddle. Those muddied clothes indicated that the youngster had done hard manual labor of some sort. The mud on them, a reddish glacial clay, was pretty strong evidence that Jimmy's flights had taken him westward into those ice-clad ranges.

A placer, a good gold placer, would fit those two facts. Perhaps Jimmy had found a placer prize and started working it, and then, unable to fight off that pack single-handed, he had whipped south for "help and a partner."

But this placer theory, good as it looked on the surface, held stumbling blocks as big as mountains. There was nothing illegal about finding a gold placer; and Jimmy had flatly stated that his work was a penitentiary offense. And why should a person keep a mining prize a secret, except just long enough to get his friends in on the ground floor? In this particular instance secrecy clashed with common sense. If Jimmy had struck any prize rich enough to account for his fight with those men, surely he or any other sane person would have staked and filed instantly. By that simple easy act he would not only have clinched his ownership but secured protection against those killers and put the whole might of the law behind himself.

"A bit of a stumper, this proposition," Noel mused, completely mystified. "I hope that these fellows kindly let me live long enough to find out what Jimmy did have up his sleeve. I'm curious."

As he was straightening up the books on the desk, he heard a footstep on the gravel outside, the door opened unexpectedly, and Harla stepped upon the threshold.

Though he nodded "Good morning" and calmly went on with his straightening up, Noel swore at this unlucky turn. Harla, of all people, catching him here! He had come early to avoid just that. Now there she stood.

One glance told him that she had slept little or none in the five hours since coming ashore. Her hand on the door latch trembled; her eyes betrayed that she had been crying; her whole manner showed that she was torn with anguish about Jimmy. She had come four thousand miles to meet him, and he was gone. Almost a month ago he had dropped out of sight, and no one had seen or heard of him since.

"What are you doing in here?" she demanded, her tones sharp with suspicion.

"I came to get a book," Noel said quietly. He picked up a weather guide in which, during his search, he had noticed Strap Barclay's name. "Strap told me to get this if I wanted it. It's his."

"Let me see that!" She came across, opened the manual to the flyleaf and glanced at Strap's name there. "It—it is his. But did it take you half an hour to step in here and get a book? I saw you come up the slope."

"I started to air this place out and tidy it up a bit," Noel explained, gentle with her, pitying her profoundly. "It was pretty stuffy, and this young fellow may be back any time; so I thought——"

"Do *you* know him?"

"Not personally. Just from what Strap said about him."

"Then how do you know he'll be back? Where is he?"

Noel hated to stir an empty hope in her, a hope which could never come true this side of eternity; but there was no help for it. He had to lull her suspicions and shield her from the truth—if he could.

"I don't know where he is," he said, "except that he's off on one of his trips. He's often gone a month or more, Strap told me. Especially during the open season, like this. But he'll be blowing in, one of these days."

Harla's eyes lighted up at this picture of Jimmy dropping down upon Manitou. But only for a moment. As she glanced at the clothes on the floor, at the dishes and other signs of hasty abandonment, her anguish came flooding back. And along with it came that suspicion which had been born in her at her first glimpse of the Diomede, on the Clearwater pier.

As Noel met her gaze across the desk, he realized that in her heart she was secretly charging *him* with Jimmy's disappearance. For the past fortnight suspicion had preyed on her till now she believed that he was one of Jimmy's enemies and knew what had happened to her brother. But still she had no absolute proof. That

Diomede, her one means of linking him to Jimmy, was sinking into the ooze of the Grand Marais, a thousand miles away.

With a visible effort she pulled herself together. "You needn't bother to straighten up this cabin. Alice and I—he and Alice are friends."

"All right," Noel agreed. He picked up the manual and walked over to the door.

As he stepped outside he debated whether or not to warn Harla about Flood. She ought to stay strictly within the post clearing during the daytime and within Alice's cabin while the twilight was on. She was so harassed about Jimmy that she was stone blind to her own danger.

But he was loath to pile another worry on her shoulders, when she was so distracted already. Likely she wouldn't heed his warning anyway. If any guarding was done, he himself would have to do it.

Passing the open window, he glanced inside the cabin. Harla's fantastic suspicion had made him impatient and a little angry, but as he looked through that window all his anger fled. Harla had picked up Jimmy's clothes and started to fold the crumpled blankets. But there she had stopped. Slumped down at the couch, with her face buried in her arms, she had broken into tears—as though she somehow knew that she had come too late to Manitou.

Back at the way-cabin, while he cooked some caribou jerky and brewed a pan of coffee. Noel decided to write a letter. As things stood, too dreadfully much depended upon himself, upon his keeping alive. If that pack should kill him—and he did not know what hour or minute it might come—this hunt would stop, Jimmy would go unavenged, and Harla would be alone here, utterly defenseless.

And there was Herm Spencer to think about, too. Herm's stolen vacation would end within a few weeks. If he came back to duty with nothing to show for his time and expense money, Superintendent Ostrand would either kick him off the Force or bust him.

A letter to Spencer, at this particular juncture, would not only safeguard the veteran sergeant but kill several other birds, at one shot.

With a mug of coffee at his elbow, he sat at the table and wrote a long code message to Herm Spencer, telling the sergeant everything about this hunt, about Harla, Flood and Jimmy. He wrote, in conclusion:

If you do not have a wireless from me by the time you receive this letter, it means that I'm out of the picture and that it's up to you and the Squad to finish this job. Select five or six of our best men and get down here on the jump. If Harla is gone, nail Flood and take any necessary measures to make him *talk*.

Noel

The letter made him feel better. If he got bumped now, Harla would have an anchor to windward, Spencer would be protected, and these men would pay for that brutal murder in Winnipeg.

Armed with the data and advice of this message, Spencer could sift into the North with a picked squad and polish off this outfit.

When he came back from the H-B store, where he unobtrusively posted his letter, he encountered a somewhat comic spectacle in front of the way-cabin. Alice Wentworth had come down there to see him; and an Indian cracky, a vicious yellow brute with a strain of wolf in it, had sprung at her and "treed" her on a granite boulder a few yards from the door. Balancing herself precariously on top of the rock, Alice was holding a paper plate in one hand and with the other was brandishing a little stick at the snarling mongrel.

"You stop that smiling," she scolded Noel, "and make this brute go away! If that dumb Policeman down there had any get-up to him, he'd shoot this yellow pug-ugly."

Noel stooped for a darnick, and the malevolent dog backed off and slunk around the cabin.

Alice stepped down from the boulder. "Thanks—lots! I was afraid every minute that my foot would slip and I'd fall right down into his teeth."

"What's that you've got in the plate?"

"A prosaic little present for you."

"Oh, a caribou steak. Fresh caribou. Don't call *that* a prosaic present. The jerky I had for breakfast was a cross between rubber and burlap." Curious, he probed: "You must be quite a Diana, Alice, to go hunting so early and bring home your caribou. Where did you go?"

"Oh, it wasn't I. It was young Paul d'Orleans, yesterday. He's Mr. Flood's hunter and guide. Mr. Flood just brought Harla and me some collops, and he thought you'd like this."

"Why, that was kind of him. I can't imagine anything better than a fresh caribou steak. Thanks for bringing this down."

After chatting a minute, Alice went back home, and Noel stepped into the way-cabin. With the plate in his hand he crossed to the south window and glanced out. Just a few feet away the vicious cracky, snarling, hackles raised, was eying a group of *métis* children at play out on the sunny slope.

"Evil and yellow and a slinker—you remind me of Frank Rocco," he said to the animal. "I sentence you, as an enemy of human happiness, to die. As your executioner, I will give you the customary good square meal beforehand. Here, take this."

Making sure that no one was looking, he tossed the fine thick steak to the dog, and then watched the animal closely.

For perhaps three minutes after wolfing the meat, the cracky showed no signs of anything wrong. With its usual viciousness it kept eying those half-breed children, eying the window where

Noel stood, and glinting around for some passer-by whom it could intimidate.

"If you're going to do any more terrorizing in your life, Rocco," Noel spoke to it, "you'd better waste no time. The last grains of sand are running out of your glass, and I don't mean perhaps. You ate Flood's little gift to me, and that's too bad for you."

Presently a sudden uneasiness struck the animal. It shook itself, growled, whirled around, and tore off down the slope, heading for the river for water.

It hardly got a hundred yards. Just inside the first willows it fell as though bowled over by a rifle bullet, and it never stirred after it fell.

For a few moments Noel stood by the window, pondering this incident and its meaning to him. Ever since Northumbria he had been plagued by a little *if*—"if Flood is my man." It had been a tiny *if* indeed, but it had existed, a tiny bothersome doubt, buzzing around and disturbing him like an irritating *brûlé* fly. It was gone now, that *if.* Through the instrumentality of an innocent girl, Flood had tried to slip him a neat quietus, and Flood had thereby given himself away.

A while later he strolled leisurely out of the cabin, vaulted upon the granite boulder, and sat there in the warm life-giving sun, smoking a philosophic pipe and watching the lazy slow-paced happenings around the little post.

There was a bit of danger in his sitting there so conspicuously, but not enough to worry him. The woods were too far away for a good rifle shot; the broad day was his friend; and just yonder at the Bay store a dozen prospectors and trappers were sunning themselves and talking "hard-rock and mus'rat."

Tonight would be a different matter.

The hour of dusk at midnight was going to be a time of crisis for him.

He knew that to his enemies he was an eyesore and worse, sitting there on that boulder and calmly smoking. They were all watching him—Flood, young d'Orleans, that nondescript pilot and the others of that pack whom he had not yet spotted. A little tingle of uneasiness was jittering through them every time they looked at him, there in the bright sun. To them he was a reminder of justice, sitting in their midst, unafraid; and embodiment of inevitable retribution, immune to anything they could do. He was sowing in their minds the small seeds of fear and eventual panic.

If he could only keep alive—and he believed he could; if he could only keep Harla from breaking up his plans—and there he had his doubts; if he could only sit tight and wait and give these men enough rope, they would hang themselves as surely as sunrise. Within this last hour Flood had made an incautious move that might conceivably have boomeranged on him.

What would the man be doing by tomorrow, and the next day and the next?

He had been sitting there just a short while when Flood came out of the Bay store and started up toward the silk tent. With deliberate purpose Noel hailed him as he passed, twenty feet out the slope.

"Hello, Flood."

Without stopping, Flood returned a friendly "Good morning, Lanier." A faint exultation was playing on his face. Plainly he was thinking that before this day was over his enemy would eat that poisoned steak and fall dead in the little way-cabin.

"Splendid day, isn't it?" Noel remarked. "And lots of day, in this country—twenty-two or - three hours. By the way, Flood——"

"Yes?"

"I hate to be a beggar, but I'm a poor hunter, myself; and besides, I lost my rifle. That fresh caribou beef——"

"Don't call it that, man," Flood interrupted, *sotto voce.* "Of course the game laws are not enforced on the Rivers, but it's just as well not to tell anybody that I gave you fresh caribou. We fellows down here call it 'wild pony,' out of season."

"I get you. Well then, the point is that I'd like to have some more wild pony, if you can spare it."

Flood frowned, perplexed. "Some more? Why, uh—surely, I'll send you more, as soon as you've disposed of——"

"Thanks a lot," Noel interrupted, very gratefully. "After all the salt fish we had on the *Midnight Sun,* that steak certainly went fine. A person would never believe that it and jerky were any relation."

Flood stopped dead-short. "What's that? You—you've—already…I mean, all of that steak—already?"

"Heavens, man, I don't make two bites of a cherry," Noel said. "Besides, I rolled breakfast and dinner into one."

He put it across so smoothly, so well padded in small talk, that Flood believed him to the last word.

"My God!" Flood jerked out, and he stared at Noel as though expecting him any instant to fall from that boulder, dead.

"What's the matter?" Noel inquired.

Flood gulped and swallowed hard and fought for self-control. "N-n-nothing. When was this—I mean, just now—you just now, uh, breakfasted, Lanier?" He seemed panicky to get away from there before his victim toppled.

"Oh no, about half an hour ago, I guess," Noel said. "I washed the dishes and have been soaking up some of this sun. Have a cigarette, Flood?"

"No, no! Thanks—thanks." A cold sweat broke out on Flood's forehead. In his confusion his face was a mirror to his thoughts. In the name of God, what manner of man was this who could eat a strychnine-salted steak *and ask for more?* "I—I've got to go. Busy today." He stooped down to recover a store purchase which had dropped from his hands; and two more packages dropped.

"Can I help with those?" Noel offered.

"No, no! Don't! You sit right there! I—I'll—I can carry them. I—I've got to go. Sorry. Busy."

He grabbed up the packages and fairly ran up the slope.

Noel watched, out of the corner of his eye. Twice Flood jerked his head around and looked back; and when he had scrambled inside his tent he whirled around and stood wide-legged behind the mosquito door, staring down at the man on the sunny boulder.

Noel smiled, a hard mirthless smile. Flood probably would figure out the truth of this matter, after a while; but meantime the man would have a bad hour, and he would *never* get back his usual jaunty assurance.

"You're not so hard to crack open, Flood," Noel apostrophized him. "You're just a slinking killer, with your poison and machine guns; and like all your tribe you're yellow."

He felt that he had Flood going, and these other men too. If he could just sit tight and wait and play a poker game with their fears, he would win in spite of having no cards worth mentioning.

A few more incidents like this caribou steak, a little more tightening of the screws, a good dose of panic with a dash of terror in it, and one of those men would come sneaking around to him with a Crown confession.

That would hang the outfit.

Around mid-afternoon, while he was preparing himself a mug-up of tea and potatoes and caribou-jerky stew, a red Bellanca with a badly spluttering engine droned into sight up south, lit splashily a thousand yards off shore and taxied in to the pier.

Strap Barclay and his mechanic, Jack Thomkins, climbed out.

Thomkins warped the Bellanca head-on against the planking, got out his tools and set to work on the motor. With dufflebag and a small locked pouch, Strap started up the slope for the way-cabin.

Noel began making more tea and slicing more jerky into a pan. In his aloneness there at Manitou it was good to have the happy-go-lucky Strap as human company. Over the little post, outwardly so peaceful and quiet, hung an air of taut expectancy that weighed on him; and he welcomed any break in the strain.

"Hello, you lucky mus'rat!" Strap greeted him, breezing in. "Say, for a nickel I'd souse you in the river. I combed that Slave muskeg for three days, last week; and wore out a motor looking for you and Harla. You stick to the main drags hereafter, or us other pilots'll strain you through a sieve."

He tossed his hat in one direction, dufflebag in another, laid the pouch on the bunk, and caught sight of the steaming bowl of stew which Noel had put on the table for himself. "Right on the dot for dinner! Dandy! Been bucking squalls and a balky engine all the way from Chipewayan, and I'm so hungry I could wipe my face with the slack in my stummick." He plopped down at the table and attacked the stew and potatoes. "This was *mine,* wasn't it? Sure it was—no fellow would ever cook up such a bum dog-feed for himself, would he? Tastes like rubber-heel goolash. But I don't mind, I'm that hungry."

"I notice. You'd better be careful with that knife—it's pretty sharp and you might cut your mouth."

"Calling me backwoods, huh? Say, fellow, I've eat in places where they'd take one look at you and wouldn't even let you in at the door."

"I don't go to those places where they look at you through the door. By the way, what's wrong with that Bellanca down there?—except the fact that it's got you for a pilot?"

"Is thaaat so? Say, if *I'd* just cracked up a ship in a mus'rat swamp, I'd keep on real low revv about other fellows' piloting. I don't know what's wrong with that motor. Jack's finding out."

"Where are you headed for, or don't you know that?"

"We're beating hell'n tanbark for Aklavik. Due there this evening with some vaccine. In that pouch. We'll play billy hell getting there before tomorrow, if Jack has to take that motor down."

"What's the trouble at Aklavik?"

"Just a coupla cases of smallpox. The Mounted has clamped on a tight quarantine, and no danger of a spread." He paused, looked up. "Say, Noel, I ran into Harla down the slope just now, and what was she driving at about that weather book?"

A little startled, Noel turned around from the stove, where he was preparing a warm meal for Thomkins. "What did she say, Strap?"

"Well, she asked me if I ever told you to get that old manual from Jimmy's cabin. She acted queer, sort of all torn up, and I didn't know what was what, so I crawfished and told her I didn't remember."

"Good. Thanks, Strap. Did she have anything else to say?"

"I hope! She blazed at me: 'You're lying. I can see it in your face.' Then she backed me up against that fur press there by the Bay, and, boy, did she read me a riot act!"

"What about?"

"That Diomede. She said: 'You saw that plane at McMurray. You know it was Jimmy's ship. Don't you lie to me!' Then she sailed into you. Said you stole that plane. Said you'd done something—she didn't know what—to Jimmy. Noel, she came an inch of saying flat-out that you put Jimmy away."

"Good Lord! What did you say to that, Strap?"

"Me? Why, I couldn't let her get by with charges like that. I stuck up for you. I was so flabbergasted that I forgot all about you telling me to keep mum. I said: 'Why, Harla, he didn't steal that plane. He bought it from Jimmy in Winnipeg——' "

Noel dropped the tin plate he was holding. "*What?* You admitted it was Jimmy's ship? Strap!"

"What's the matter, partner? Did I spill some beans for you?"

"It—it's all right, I guess," Noel managed, badly jarred by this calamitous turn. Harla knew now, at last, that the plane *had* been Jimmy's. At last she had positive proof linking him to her brother. Her suspicions now had something solid to go on.

He wondered what her next move would be.

He was not personally afraid of those suspicions. At any time he could blow them to pieces with a word. But he *was* afraid for his hunt. All day he had been telling himself, "If I can only keep Harla out of this." Now he could not possibly keep her out. She was going to force his hand. When she did, good-bye to this cool promising game he was playing.

CHAPTER ELEVEN

IN the windy darkness Noel heard, or thought he heard, cautious footsteps on the gravel path out the slope. The sound seemed to be drawing nearer.

His hand tightened on his automatic, and he listened closely.

In the certain knowledge that within this hour Flood was going to loose calamity at him, he had got out of the way-cabin into the safety of the night. But he had not gone far—he wanted to watch the place and see what happened. Sitting in lee of the boulder where he had sunned himself that day, he was waiting in the dark and wondering what brand of annihilation Flood would try this time.

A small storm, mostly wind but with an occasional spatter of rain and sleet, had blown in from the Arctic Ocean that evening. The thick pall of clouds scudding out of the north had brought on the twilight earlier than usual; and the dark was intense.

He was glad of the storm. The heavy wind had waked up the Mackenzie; the waves were too rough for Flood's Albatross to get away; and so Harla was reasonably safe tonight.

Down at the wharf, Strap and Thomkins, spurred on by an urgent wireless from Aklavik, were hard at work on the Bellanca radial, by the light of candle-lanterns and a spluttering blow-torch. Except for a glow in Alice Wentworth's cabin, the little post was dark and asleep.

In the rain and gloom, Noel's thoughts had drifted back to that happy evening at McMurray—the soda, shanty dance and Harla's warm instinctive friendliness. He had not dreamed, then, that hardly a fortnight later he would be battling to forget her so that he might have peace at heart again. With half a chance he and Harla could have been the best of friends and partners. If she hated him now, if her emotional attitude was irretrievably warped and ruined, the blame lay squarely with this damnable hunt. That lost friendship was the price which he himself was personally paying for Flood's crime.

For a few seconds after that first scrunch on the gravel, he heard nothing more. Then he caught the noise again, closer, coming in his direction—the unmistakable sound of footsteps.

Somebody was sneaking up to the way-cabin, thinking to find him asleep there.

He flattened himself against the rock and waited, hoping that the intruder would not lose nerve but would walk boldly inside and flash a light on that bunk in the corner. With a sleeping poke, a pair of boots and a blanket, he had made a dummy of himself on that bunk. It was a good job, cunning and deceptive, with those boots protruding lifelike from the blanket, and even a mosquito veil over the "face." This intruder, probably nervous already, would take one look at the dummy, pour a magazine of bullets into it, whirl away and get out of there—and report to Flood that their enemy had been killed so instantly that he had not even stirred.

With a bit of grim amusement Noel anticipated the scene tomorrow morning when he would walk out of that cabin into the sun, and stagger Flood with a nonchalant "Hello, friend," and clamp his vise a little tighter on the man.

Out of the gusty blackness the intruder loomed up, dimly, and drew near the boulder, and passed it, and with slow hesitant steps moved on toward the cabin.

As the dark figure went by him, almost within arm's reach, Noel caught a faint odor on the rain-sweet air. The odor of perfume.

Fairly stunned, he rose up and stared through the windy darkness at the dim figure. In kaleidoscopic flashes that perfume brought him memories of the McMurray dance, of Harla beside him in the Diomede, of their day in the cramped rock-niche.

"Not Harla!" he breathed. "It can't be. She wouldn't visit me if she and I were alone on the moon."

But he knew that the person *was* Harla; and this midnight visit of hers so bewildered him that he left the boulder and followed her to the cabin.

When Harla reached the door, he was only a couple of paces behind her. His intention was to speak to her and get her away from there instantly. That way-cabin was dangerous. Flood's blow might fall at any minute. A stick of dynamite with short fuse, whirring through door or window—that was just one of several possibilities.

But Harla's actions were so queer, this whole visit so strange and puzzling, that he kept silent and watched her.

On the threshold Harla snapped on a flashlight, and shifted the yellow beam from one to another of the three bunks till it rested upon the one in the corner.

The flash cast a feeble periphery of light upon her own self; and by that wan glow Noel saw that she was trembling all over and was so wobbly that she leaned against the door for steadiness. The flashlight shook in her hand; the yellow beam jiggered and danced. And she was crying—the suppressed broken sobs of a person on the very brink of collapse.

He realized that something cataclysmic had happened to her within the past two hours. Something had hit and overwhelmed her like a mile-long slide. Anxiety or worry did not explain this heartbroken sobbing. Only one thing could have knocked her reeling like this. *She had found out that Jimmy was dead.* Somebody had told her.

That person was Flood. No one else, not even Strap, knew about that night in Winnipeg. Through his visits to the

Wentworth cabin Flood had got to Harla. Some time this evening, for some unknown purpose, he had tumbled that tragic news upon her. Not gently, not with pity and compassion, but with brutal abruptness.

"Well, she knows now," Noel thought, and his arms dropped in a little gesture of disaster. Ever since McMurray he had fought to shield her from that knowledge. His attempt to keep her out of this battle had cost him his pride, tangled him in a mass of lies, lost him Harla's friendship, steeled her against him; and now that whole cruel price had gone for nothing. Futile, all of it.

He cursed at this ruinous blow to his plans. Just when he had maneuvered himself into good position and was clamping the screws to those men, his fine strategy was suddenly undermined and toppling.

As Harla left the door and stumbled over to the middle of the cabin, he saw a large jeweled revolver in her right hand and saw that the flash was pointing straight at the corner bunk where lay the dummy of himself. Not until that moment did he grasp Harla's reason for this strange visit. But the gun and yellow shaft told him her purpose. More forcefully than any words.

"My God, she's gunning for *me!*"

There was a little space, a few seconds, when he himself leaned against that door for steadiness. The realization of Harla's purpose was like a slow knife sliding home. He shrank back from believing it; he tried to shove it away and deny it out of existence. But he could neither deny nor doubt. That gun was meant for him. He shut his eyes, to blot out the sight of Harla standing there with that glittering revolver in her hand; but he saw her still.

He whirled on his heel, to get away from that cabin. He was suddenly weary of this thankless hunt and wanted to quit it cold. His month of danger and heavy sacrifice had brought him this—Harla and that jeweled gun. His watchful guard over her, his love, his costly silence, his compassion for her tragedy—it had all come down to this end, that Harla considered him a person of evil and wished him dead.

But as he turned away from that threshold, he checked himself. "Can't leave her here, in this danger," he thought, doggedly. "Got to get her out of this cabin and back to hers. And then——"

He felt no anger against Harla personally. The girl's heart was a chaos. She had been victimized. The guilt lay with Flood. Taking advantage of her anguished distraction, Flood had told her and *convinced* her that the man in the way-cabin had slain her brother and stolen the little Diomede.

But the fact remained that Harla stood there with gun in hand, a gun meant for him; and that fact had devastating consequences within himself. Abrupt consequences, like a light going out. In a vague fashion he realized that this "visit" of hers was a mercy bullet, putting an end to his whole sorry attempt to win her. Henceforth he could not possibly have anything more to do with Harla DeLong in a friendly way, and henceforth she would have no power to hurt him.

A shower of icy rain swept across the clearing and drummed on the cabin roof and beat against him, as he waited for the bark of that gun. Oblivious to it, he glanced out at the dark slope, listened, turned toward Harla. Why didn't she shoot? What was stopping her?

The revolver glittered as she raised the weapon and pointed it at the bunk. A violent shudder swept through her, and her gun hand fell to her side.

In spite of his desperate impatience, he silently watched her. Why didn't she squeeze that trigger? Courage? She had plenty. But something was stopping her, all right. Three times, now, she had raised the revolver, and each time her hand had dropped.

He fancied he knew what was knocking that revolver down. When Harla came right up to the point of shooting him, her instinctive judgment balked. Flood's poisonous lie, the Diomede and the other damning evidence against him had brought her here; but that was the farthest wash of the wave. Her instincts were sounder than her reason. Her instincts were telling her that the man who had shielded her with his own body from that machine gun and had risked his life to bring her a drink of water, was not a man of evil.

That was why she could lift and aim the gun and yet could not squeeze the trigger.

From the open clearing, a hundred yards up slope, came the muffled hoot of an owl. The macaber sound jolted Noel. Owls didn't sit around on grassy slopes or hoot while on wing. That call came from the lips of a man. It was some signal between his enemies. Those men were abroad on this dark slope. Flood must have been listening for Harla's shot, and failed to hear any, and knew she had not carried through.

At the moment when he whirled again toward Harla, the gun fell from her hand and clattered on the rough slab floor. As she clasped at the table to keep from falling, the flash dropped, and the cabin went dark.

"Noel, Noel"—she had broken completely down and was sobbing aloud—"how could you do that—to him? ... He was all I had—my brother—Jimmy——"

Noel hurried across to her, quickly, and steadied her, his arm around her waist. "Harla! Come with me. Let's get out of here!"

She recognized his voice. Noel felt her shudder when he touched her. She tried to push him away.

"You fool!"—he cracked the words at her like a whiplash, to rouse her, because the seconds were precious. And to keep her from fighting against him, he snapped out. "I'm your friend. I was Jimmy's. I'm hunting the men who killed Jimmy. Do you understand *that?* Stop crying. No questions now. Come along. Hurry it!"

He started to lead her toward the door, but she swayed and stumbled, and she was altogether too slow to suit him, what with those hoot-owls on the slope. He simply picked her up in his arms, carried her out of the way-cabin into the windy night, carried her on past the boulder to the fish scaffolding forty yards beyond.

There, in the blackness, he stopped with her.

"We were lucky to slip them," he whispered. "As soon as it's safe, I'll take you up to Alice's cabin, and I'll watch the place myself while this dark is on. In an hour or two, when you're a bit steadier, I'd like to talk with you, Harla. You know some facts about Jimmy that I must have."

No answer. Only that heartbroken sobbing.

Still carrying her, he groped in beneath some lean-to planks where they were sheltered from the icy rain, and sat down with her on an old abandoned birchbark.

"Harla, please—those men are around. They might hear you." He smoothed back her disheveled hair and petted her as one might a child, to let her know that at least she had one friend in her black hour. She seemed so lost, so hopelessly bewildered in all this tangle of his falsehoods and Flood's lies; she seemed groping help-lessly in a blackness like this storm-lashed night ... He believed that for her to know the truth about this hunt might bring her a little way out of chaos and put her feet on firmer ground.

In cautious whispers he began talking to her, while he kept glancing around in the dark and listening for sinister footsteps. Not in self-defense—he no longer cared greatly about that—but to stop her from crying and to win, perhaps later, a little coöpera-tion from her, he began telling her of that Winnipeg night and of how a wanton laugh had brought him into this far North, a shadow trailing shadows ....

A candleglow had appeared in Flood's tent.

As Noel sat through the spatters of rain and sleet, watch-ing Alice's cabin while the one-o'clock dawn came slowly on, he glanced up slope occasionally at that glow and struggled with the temptation to go up there and kill the man.

Because of Flood, inside that cabin a girl was crying her heart out, behind that drawn blind. Because of Flood, young Jimmy, down in Winnipeg—a splendid young life cut off... And how much other wreckage lay scattered back along this man's years only the devil's bookkeeper knew.

To slip up to that silk tent and do a private piece of work on Flood would be easy enough; and *he* could get by with it. With one little bullet he could make sure that Flood would wreck no more innocent people's lives. Here was a clean-cut chance to get Flood before the man got him or Harla or both of them.

But for all his temptation and his seething fury at Flood, he refused to walk those hundred steps and end his hunt.

It was not fear or conscience that kept him sitting there in the rain, but a vague hunch.

For days he had been wondering where Raphael Flood had come from. A person of Flood's caliber did not spring out of nowhere. Flood had a background. What was it? What was he doing here in the North? Had his feud with Jimmy been the whole picture or merely a part of a larger canvas? Was this man an international adventurer? Or a person of two lives—a Jekyll and Hyde? Or what?

To these questions he had no answer; but he was convinced that he had flushed big game, in the person of Raphael Flood. This hunt was no mere man-hunt, as he had imagined at the start, but something of depths and unpredictable possibilities. More or less accidentally he had stumbled onto a case which might pack more high explosive than the Rocco affair itself.

Besides his chance to wipe out the stinging disgrace of that hunt, the mere thought of working on a case of national importance stirred all the bloodhound in his nature. Trailing and putting away obscure individual criminals seemed so futile and endless. Like plugging up rat holes that would be dug open the minute a person turned his back. Or like knocking over poisonous toadstools when a new crop was certain to spring up with the next rain.

But a case which had impact on a nation and exercised a widespread power for good, was a different matter. That struck at the roots of crime, by driving home a lesson. Those major cases come but rarely, two or three in a lifetime. To handle one of them successfully was an accomplishment of enduring worth.

While the gray dawn broadened, he mapped out a line of action for himself. Providing he could manage Harla and keep her from ruining his plans, he would explore this case thoroughly before breaking it open. Would dig into Flood. Find out who the man was. His background. His criminal hook-ups. And when he did have the goods on Flood, he would take the man back to civilization *alive*. No more "gallant deaths" or maudlin sentiment over a dead criminal....

When he stepped into the Wentworth cabin, near one-thirty, he met Alice in the outer room. All excited and wrought up, the girl started pouring questions at him.

"Are you really Inspector Irving? That's what Harla said. She's been saying it over and over. And this about Jimmy—that can't be true! *Is* it true? It's all so dreadful. I can't believe that Mr. Flood had any hand——"

Noel cut her short. "It'll be worse than dreadful if you tell anybody what you've seen and heard here tonight." He had little patience with the girl; she had fallen for Flood too easily, on the *Midnight Sun*. With a sharpness that shocked and awed her, he snapped: "I want you to forget everything you know about this— who I am, Harla, Jimmy, everything. That's orders. I particularly don't want you to see Flood or exchange one single word with him. If you disobey, you'll find yourself arrested for obstructing justice."

Alice paled. "I'll do as you say," she agreed, and Noel saw she meant it. "I won't see Mr. Flood and I won't talk."

Noel relented with her. "That's good. Sometime you'll thank me for that order." He motioned at the small north room of the cabin. "Will she talk to anyone?"

"Yes. I was just in."

Noel crossed to the room and stepped into the tiny bedroom.

By the dim candle on Alice's dresser he saw Harla lying on the couch, motionless, her face turned to the wall. She seemed to have cried herself out. She was very quiet—when he came in she did not look around or move.

Across the foot of the couch lay Alice's small bore rifle, a half-filled clip of cartridges and a carton of shells partly spilled on the blanket. Some time during the past hour Harla had evidently got up, secured the weapon and made a pitiable attempt to load it.

The rifle and cartridges were no surprise to Noel. Mute symbol of Harla's blind reckless vengeance, they merely warned him that he was in for trouble in managing her. A few hours more, till she pulled herself together, and the proverbial wild horses could not hold her.

He stepped over and sat down on the edge of the couch. He felt that he could really be a friend to Harla now, after what had happened within him in that way-cabin. An unselfish and stern friend, stern for her own good. He was looking back across his relationship with her as one would look back across a wretched journey which one has finished. With regret for what it might have been; with relief that it was over. He was no longer butting his head against a stone wall. He no longer hoped or wished for her friendship. That hope had snapped.

"Harla, will you talk to me?"

Harla turned and looked up at him, and Noel saw that she was thinking of her "visit" to the way-cabin. Her pale cheeks slowly colored. In her eyes he saw a shame and humiliation such as he had seldom seen in any human.

"Harla, forget it," he said gently. "We all make mistakes. Your mistake was almost inevitable, under the circumstances. Let's bury it and never recur to it again."

She managed, falteringly: "It's not so easy as that Noel. *I* can't bury it." She gazed at him questioningly, as though noticing his change toward her and trying to fathom it. "You despise me now, don't you, Noel?"

"You're awfully headlong in your conclusions, girl. First you think I'm a decent sort, then you think I'm a criminal and worse, then you think I despise you—— I wonder what will come next. As a matter of fact, I admire your courage for coming down there. Flood wouldn't ever have done it. In a showdown you've got more nerve than he or any of his men. And I admire your good sense in knowing, all along, that I was lying to you about myself. Now, let's get down to business. Harla, what was Jimmy doing here in the North? Did he let you in on his secret?"

"Yes, Noel. It was a placer, a gold placer."

"What? A placer? Are you sure about this?"

"I'm sure. He wrote me that it was a small pocket but very, very rich. He said that the concentration ran higher than Fraser's Cradle, in the Golden Caribou."

"Where's it located?"

"I don't know."

"Why didn't he stake and file?"

"I wondered about that, too, Noel. I asked him why he didn't, but he wouldn't answer that question."

"How could his placer be illegal? Why was he afraid of the penitentiary?"

His words astonished Harla. "Penitentiary, illegal—was it that? Did Jimmy say that to you?"

Her question showed Noel that except for this one central fact of the placer she knew as little as he himself about Jimmy's venture. Probably because of this penitentiary angle Jimmy had kept silent to her.

"That must have been the reason," Harla said, "why he wouldn't let me join him. I wanted to get a leave of absence and come, but he said no. But when he wrote about these enemies, I came anyway. I thought I could keep him out of danger. He was so headstrong and impulsive, and didn't know it."

Under any other circumstances Noel would have smiled at those words, from her. Headstrong, impulsive—the pot was calling the kettle black.

Though Harla seemed positive about this placer business, he himself was dubious. Why Jimmy hadn't staked, how his prize could possibly be illegal—those two objections were still as mountainous as ever. Maybe Jimmy had not told Harla the truth.

He put the tantalizing question aside. Just now his job was to handle Harla. She would wreck his whole program unless he could head her off. She had the courage of any man, she was a deadly shot, and she was wild with vengeance. She would either kill Flood or get killed herself.

"Harla," he said, "our goal is to settle up for Jimmy, isn't it? We must make Flood and his outfit pay. The burden of the job falls on me, as a trained professional. But you can help. In fact, you may be the difference between winning and losing.

"It's like this. I'm alone, here at Manitou; I'm up against, a brainy pack of killers; and there's the hard job of building a court-sure case against them. It takes a lot of evidence to put a noose around a man's neck. In other words, I've got my hands full to keep myself alive and hang those men."

Harla saw what was coming. "You want me to go away. You don't want the burden of keeping me alive too."

"That's about it. I'll arrange with Strap to take you south. When he comes back from Aklavik he can pick you up."

Harla stopped him. "He won't pick me up, because I won't go."

Her firm tones dismayed Noel. She spoke with such deadly quietness. That "won't" was as hard as a cannon ball.

She went on: "Noel, if you stay here, all alone, you'll just get killed and Flood will get away. You haven't got a shred of evidence against him and you never will have. You yourself told me that those men left no tracks. You know and I know who's guilty. Why dig around for evidence? Or why run the risk that a court will turn these men free? Or why *wait?*"

Noel bore down hard on her. "Harla, you're being a hotheaded fool. You, a girl, with no training or experience, throwing yourself against a pack like this—it's suicide. And not only that, but you'll spike my chances if you stay. You've got to go."

His words bounced off of Harla like pebbles from a boulder. She had a mind of her own, and she had made it up.

"I'm not going, Noel. Please don't argue. I don't want you to protect me. I'll look out for myself. And I'm not asking you to—to go outside the law. This is *my* fight. He was my brother."

Her refusal left Noel floundering. He had planned on her going back south; had staked all his hopes on that. But she would never go. He saw this so clearly that he dropped the argument.

In the silence between them he reached out surreptitiously for the rifle clip and cartridges, and slipped them into his pocket. Anything to halt her and hold her, if only for a few hours—till he could scheme some other way of freezing her out of this.

"You're making a bad mistake in staying here," he warned, as he got up to go. "I only hope that you don't regret it too bitterly."

In the outer room, as he left, he bade Alice: "Try to keep her in this cabin till I have a chance to cook up something. I thought I could manage her, but I found out different."

He gave Alice the clip and cartridges. "Hide these where she can't find them. And hide that jeweled revolver. If she starts on any rampage that you can't handle, come down and get me."

CHAPTER TWELVE

SHORTLY after sun-up, Strap Barclay, grimy and tired from his all-night job on the Bellanca motor, trudged into the way-cabin, where Noel was trying to catch a little rest.

"Say, Noel, this Constable Brannigan, the bush cop here at Manitou, has got a pretty kittle of fish on his hands. You'd better ankle down to the Police building and give him a lift. He's hopping around like a chicken with its head off."

Noel wearily turned to the wall. "I'm not ankling anywhere. I've got a kettle of fish of my own."

Strap poured himself a mug of coffee. "Get off that bunk and do what I tell you. Brannigan's a jackass, and this trouble is serious. You're the only bozo around here with a pint of brains, except myself, and I've got to beat hell-for-leather for Aklavik. Come on, let's have some revv out of you."

"What's up?"

"Plenty. Back here in the Silvertip Mountains there's a band of Smokies in devilish hard lines, the poor skites. A young runner just got in to Manitou with the news. Something's got to be done, and fast, or there'll be billy hell to pay. These Dinokuis'll get completely wiped out, and not only that but——"

Noel turned around again. "Dinokuis?" He was so tired that it took him a moment or two to realize that these were the "queer tall Indians" in whom Harla was interested. "What's the trouble with them?"

Between gulps of black coffee Strap sketched him the story which the young runner had brought out of the northwestern mountains. Ten days ago a strange sickness had broken out among the Dinokuis—a devastating sickness against which their ancestral herbs and shaman potents were powerless. A dozen of the band were already dead, and half the others were dangerously ill. Some of the men, panic-stricken, were on the verge of fleeing the camp and leaving the Dinokui range.

On his hundred-and-fifty mile trip to Manitou for help, the young runner, one of the few Dinokuis who had ever had contact with white people, had taken sick himself; but he had fought on and on and finally stumbled in to the post, an hour ago.

"I'll bet a leg it's smallpox," Strap concluded. "Been several little flare-ups along the Three Rivers this season. The police always throw in a detail and localize it. But if those Dinokui men pitch off from camp, they'll spread this to the Yukon-iho-Tenneh and the coast Eskimos; and that *will* be a kittle of fish! Any little thing, even measles, mows these Smokies down like flies."

Noel sat up on the bunk and tried to shake off his weariness. Besides the humanity of the thing, that strange old tribe ought to be saved, if possible, because of their worth to anthropology. There were other Indians but no other Dinokuis.

Strap brought him some coffee. "Here, swallow this, and we'll ankle."

As Strap and he went down the slope, the suspicion struck him that this Indian's account might be another of Flood's deadfalls for him. But when they pushed through the gaping crowd at the Police cabin and stepped inside, he found that the story was all too true. The young Dinokui, a mere boy of nineteen, was lying huddled on a cot, limp with exhaustion and half delirious with fever.

Noel bent over him, took one good look, straightened up and nodded to Strap. "You hit it. Smallpox, all right."

Constable Brannigan, a raw recruit from the "Awkward Squad" at Regina, had dosed the young Indian promiscuously from the medicine chest; and now, at a table, he was laboriously scratching away with pen and paper, making out a lengthy report to his Officer Commanding at Fort James.

Noel stepped across to him. "Constable, it'll be ten days or two weeks before that report of yours gets to Fort James. This is a crisis, and the hours count."

The distracted constable swung around. "Who asked you to come butting in? I've gotta make a written report, haven't I? In ink! That's Manual orders, ain't it? Whadda you know about Mounted Police work?"

"Nothing, friend; nothing at all," Noel assured. "But why don't you send your O-C a wireless? As things stand, you're responsible for whatever happens here; but the minute you get word to him, you're out from under, and he's responsible."

Brannigan's eyes popped open. "Why—why that's so. I'll do it! What'll I tell the O-C?"

"I'll write your wire," Noel suggested.

He leaned over, penciled a message to Inspector Clevenger and handed it to Brannigan. "Here—sign this and tell the wireless man to click it through and get a confirm on it."

Brannigan grabbed his hat and hurried out the door. Noel stepped back to the Indian boy and looked down at him, thoughtfully. It would be tomorrow before a Police detail could reach Manitou, with supplies and medicine and a doctor. In the meanwhile, that stricken camp, the terrific danger that those men might flee, might scatter this sickness far and wide——

He turned to Strap. "Do you know the way across to this Dinokui camp?"

"Gosh, no! Those Silvertips are the devil's own hangout."

"Some of those men out there must know."

"They don't. I asked. Nobody ever goes back into those ranges. The Police plane'll have to follow the Dinokui River, I guess, and try to spot the camp smoke."

The young Indian heard them and tried to sit up. "Want guide, huh? Tah-Gomaugh go 'long, show where camp, do the back-and-forth talk." Too sick even to lean on his elbow, he slumped back upon the cot.

"That boy's got stuff," Strap remarked. "Imagine whooping across those mountains when you're that near caving in. If he hadn't taken it on his own hook to come for help, we wouldn't know anything about this trouble. He's pretty sick, Noel. D'you believe he'll keep till tomorrow?"

"He should. He's a fighter. But this delay—I don't like it. Strap, you ought to whip across to that camp. A hundred and fifty miles is only an hour's hop."

"Man, I can't! I'm overdue at Aklavik now."

"You and the Bellanca and your vaccine are needed worse at this camp than at Aklavik. Aklavik's got two cases and a Police quarantine, and back there are fifty cases and not a soul around. Why don't you take Thomkins and Brannigan, take that vaccine, rake together what medicine you can, and get over there? You could straighten the camp up a bit and stop those men from leaving. Tomorrow may be too late."

"I like that—loading it all onto me. What's the matter with your going along? I don't know anything about vaccine or medicines."

"I can't go, Strap. I can't leave Manit——"

He bit the word off short, with an idea volting through his brain. Here was deliverance, like a miracle, laid in his very hands, and he had almost tossed it away. If he should put his own plans temporarily on the shelf and go across to that camp, he could persuade Harla to go along with him. He could get her away from Manitou. He'd get her over there, get her busy, pry her mind away from Flood and Jimmy. When the Police detail arrived, so that she would be safe, he could quietly return to Manitou and set to work on Flood undisturbed, with Harla completely sidetracked!

"Of course I'll go, Strap. My brain was just foggy, and I couldn't think straight. We'll have room for Harla?"

"Sure. The Bellank's a six-placer. Think she'll go?"

"She'll go if we have to kidnap her!"

"Dandy! She knows Smokies from A to Z, and besides she can sort of take over the women and kids."

"Right. So let's have some of that revv. Go and tell Thomkins to get the Bellanca warm. Then come back here and rake this medicine together. I'll prop this young Indian up with a hypo and then I'll get Harla. Let's be in the air in twenty minutes."

Through the plane window Noel gazed down at the mountains under keel, at the appalling panorama of ice and snow and rock; and he understood why the Dinokui Indians had come down through the centuries without being swamped by the neighboring Tenneh tribes. With no trails or canoe streams leading in, the country was impossible to any creature without wings. The Silvertips were no orderly range but a huge jumble of individual mountains; the canyon-narrow valleys were impenetrably choked with buckbrush and tremendous talus slides.

From the valley depths the banksian pines climbed only a few thousand feet up the slopes. Above the last straggle of timber lay gleaming-white *névés,* cold and sparkling in the morning sun. Above the *névés* sprawled fields of flinty-blue ice—half a hundred glaciers within the sweep of his eyes; and high above ice and snow reared the naked pinnacle summits, stark rock masses towering nearly three miles into the sky.

Off to the north he caught occasional glimpses of the Dinokui River, plunging and stair-stepping out of the mountains to fling itself into the slow Mackenzie. Its galloping white waters and thundering overfalls made it look like a canoeist's nightmare, a river to hurl back the boldest of northern prospectors.

In the mechanic's place beside Strap, young Tah-Gomaugh, wrapped in blankets and braced up with a strychnine hypodermic, was guiding the Bellanca straight northwest across that savage country to the Dinokui camp. The icy winds and treacherous air chasms kept Strap busy, as he skimmed low over the glacier fields and sailed high above the canyon-valleys. In the rear place beside Thomkins; Constable Brannigan sat hunched over the medicine chest, so frightened by the wild region and the fifteen-thousand-foot height that he had pulled his hat down and would not look out.

Occasionally Noel glanced at Harla, beside him, and was glad for her sake that this cold bumpy flight would soon be over. She looked very tired—nearly exhausted by all she had gone through in the stormy hours past. Her eyelids drooped heavily and she was unconsciously leaning against his shoulder. Apparently she had no suspicion that he had tricked her and was marooning her in these mountains till he finished with Flood.

She seemed almost a totally different girl from the Harla DeLong who had sat beside him on the Diomede flight. Then he had clothed her with hope and wish, but that had dropped now, and he could regard her with impersonal detachment. For that he was glad. No more snubbings or bitter disappointments or suspicions that cut like a whip. A day at this Dinokui camp, possibly a day or two later on at Manitou, and then their trails would separate. And for that too he was glad. He felt that only when he was many months and half a continent away from her could he really begin to forget.

Through the wispy cirrus clouds a great bowl-shaped basin in the mountains loomed up ahead. Nearly thirty miles long and twenty wide, the basin was like a low sheltered amphitheater—an area of verdant green in an immensity of ice and snow. From a big moraine lake on northwest the Dinokui River coiled down through the middle of that beautiful valley.

A peaceful blue stream there, the river seemed to be taking a deep quiet breath before its mad canyon dash to the Mackenzie.

The Bellanca sped nearer, and the valley opened up wider, sunlit and lovely. Protected from winter storms, walled in against marauding Tenneh tribes, the lush basin looked like as fine a hunting grounds as any Indian heart could wish. What a sanctuary, centuries ago, to that lost and wandering band of old Algonquins. Little wonder that they had stayed there, down across the ages.

The isolation of the place made him question how a sickness of the contagious type could have broken out among the Dinokuis.

The flare-ups along the much-traveled Three Rivers were understandable, but this one was a puzzler. Nobody ever came back into this region.

Not a person there at Manitou had ever set foot on the Dinokui range.

The Bellanca swam in between two towering pinnacles and tilted sharply downward into the basin. Tah-Gomaugh pointed at the southeastern end of the valley, at a mid-river island surrounded by a flock of small islets like a duck with an argosy of fledglings.

"Camp there," he grunted.

As the plane dropped down in whistling spirals, Noel saw two thin threads of campfire smoke standing up from the pine-clad island; and then the Dinokui village took on outline. Covering about five acres, the village was laid out with geometric precision, in form of an oblong; and from the air its pattern seemed true to the inch. A wide stone wall enclosed the whole place. Within the wall were two semi-circles of buildings; and in the exact middle was a huge cross, of flat stonework.

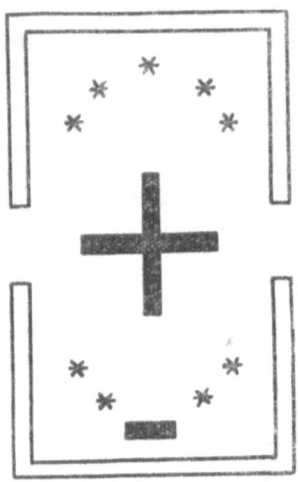

The sight of the village had roused Harla from her weariness. Gripping Noel's arm in excitement, she was gazing down, wide-eyed, staring first from one window and then the other as the plane spiraled.

"Noel! Look! *Stone houses!* And look—on those little islets—at those rock mounds! Those are burial cairns. Look at their designs—fish and bird and animal! Noel, look!"

He was thankful for her excitement. Flood and Jimmy and Manitou were temporarily crowded out of her mind. "But heaven pity me," he thought, "when and if she wakes up and realizes I tricked her. She'll probably use me for target practice before she goes after Flood."

As the Bellanca glided over the village at five hundred feet, he saw that one of the smoke threads came from a cluster of small dwellings in the upper part of the village. The other smoke rose from a large circular house, half underground and roofed with logs, in the lower semi-circle. From what Tah-Gomaugh had told him at Manitou, he knew that the large structure was the men's *kozgee* or ceremonial hall, where the men had gathered and were going through their rituals to appease the evil Familiars.

Strap set the Bellanca down skillfully and taxied into the shallows, within a rod of the landwash.

From the *kozgee* a dozen men and from the dwellings some fifty-odd women and children had come out into the sun, and were staring in wordless consternation at the huge bird-beast which had thundered out of the sky and descended upon their village. But none of them fled or picked up weapons or even moved. The red death striking and striking at them had so dazed them with grief that they cared little about anything else.

From the open cabin door Noel looked the village over, planning what to do. Hard-hit though it was, the camp was not nearly so stricken as he had feared. A good part of the band were still well, and most of the sick ones were able to stagger around. The contagion seemed to have taken one of its queer turns here and was running a mild varioloid course. If it had struck with its usual deadliness among Indians, there would hardly be a soul alive of this band.

He gave instructions:

"Strap, you and Thomkins patrol this island and see that nobody leaves it. Keep a special watch on those birchbark canoes across yonder. I noticed that a dozen of them are loaded with food and weapons, ready to go. Some time toward evening you two will have to whip back to Manitou, so that you can guide Clevenger's Police detail in. Brannigan, you tote the supplies ashore and stand by to help Harla. She'll take the upper half of this camp, and I'll look after the men.

"Harla, we'll get these people out of those dank smoky houses into the warm fresh air. Then we'll vaccinate. Then we'll see about medicine and food. They're all demoralized here. From the looks of things, they haven't had anything to eat in days. But first, you and I had better take Tah-Gomaugh ashore and establish diplomatic relations."

He carried the sick Tah-Gomaugh through the shallows; and with the young Indian between them, he and Harla walked up a black stone path to the center of the cross.

"Stop here," Tah-Gomaugh bade, uneasy, a bit uncertain about the welcome that his people were going to give his white friends.

As Noel stared around at the queer stone houses, the cooking pits, the ritual "sun stones," the crude pottery and primitive artifacts of this primitive band, an eerie sensation, weird, almost frightening, crept over him. The whole scene around him seemed unreal—touched with the strangeness of magic. He felt he was standing in an old stone town of a Stone-Age folk; that in coming from that airplane up the black stone path to this abode of a hunting and fishing people, he had walked out of the modern present, walked back across history and human progress into an ancient Mound-builder village, exactly as Harla once had said.

The Dinokui men and women left the *kozgee* and dwellings and dwellings and came near, and Tah-Gomaugh called to them, repeating some guttural phrase over and over. With no sign either of friendliness or hostility, they kept coming closer till they stood in a circle around Noel and Harla.

Tall and muscular, with coarse black hair and red-copper skin, they looked to Noel not unlike modern Crees or Assiniboines of pure stock. The men, bare from the waist up, wore caribou-leather trousers and pointed moccasins, and carried daggers of black obsidian at their belts. The women were clad in shirt and trousers of some whitish skin; their quilled moccasins were dyed a pretty vermilion; and all of them wore hammer-wrought ornaments of raw virgin silver.

After staring sharply at Noel and listening to Tah-Gomaugh's explanations, one of the men, apparently a *tyee* or chief, raised his hand and gave a little harangue to the rest of the group.

"What did he say, Tah-Gomaugh?" Noel asked, trying to shake off the eerie dreamlike feeling which lay upon him.

"He say you welcome. He say you come as friend. How know? He say no man take his squaw long on war trail."

Though the *tyee's* premise was somewhat askew, Noel was vastly relieved at his conclusion.

"Tell them," he bade Tah-Gomaugh, "that we have medicine for their sickness. Tell those who are still well that we are going to vaccinate them so that——"

Harla spoke up: "They'll never understand that, Noel. Medicine and vaccine mean nothing to them." She instructed Tah-Gomaugh: "Tell them that we have little boxes full of powerful magic. Tell them that the sorcerers of the white man have fashioned a hollow needle filled with *friendly* Familiars and that the needle's burning point will let those Familiars into their blood. Tell them they should come out of their houses; that the evil Familiars of their sickness are withered by the Lord Sun."

She turned to Noel. "That's the way you've got to talk to get across. Everything that you do here, make a ritual of it. And don't break into any of their superstitions. If we appear to be forcing alien ideas on them, they'll likely blame the very next death on us and drive us away."

In the Dinokui tongue, sounding mostly like clicks and grunts, Tah-Gomaugh began speaking to them as Harla had instructed. Watching their reactions, Noel speedily saw that her approach to them was the dead-right approach. They understood this talk about magic and Familiars. Crowding closer, they listened with bated breath; and their faces, weary and haggard, lit up with a new hope, with a childlike faith that their visitors' magic would deliver them.

Even before Tah-Gomaugh finished speaking, one of the younger women, carrying in her arms a little tot of three, evidently her first-born, stepped out of the group and came up to Harla, touched Harla's arm and pointed at the child, and said something in low imploring voice. Noel knew that she was begging Harla to save the tot. Though the woman was so sick that she could scarcely stand, she asked nothing for herself, no help or magic—only a healing touch for her child.

For Noel the incident snapped the tension of the queer scene and surroundings. The dream-quality of the old stone village faded. The odd people around him became men and women who were little different, at heart, from himself and Harla and all the rest of mankind. A mother asking that her child be saved— that was universal humanity speaking, a humanity common throughout the lands of the earth and back across the centuries of history.

CHAPTER THIRTEEN

FOR twelve hours on end, without rest and with only a few bites to eat, Noel plowed through one task after another, down at his part of the village.

After much persuasion he induced the men to leave the dark chill *kozgee;* and under the pines behind it he set up an open-air camp, making pallets of pine boughs and bighorn robes. With elaborate ritual he vaccinated all those who had not yet taken sick. He talked Tah-Gomaugh's older brother and another man into stooping to "squaw work," and had them prepare caribou broth and other proper food at one of the cooking pits.

Though he was saving human lives, he begrudged every hour and minute of that day. He wanted to be back on the Mackenzie, pushing his fight against Flood. In this interval Flood might slip him and vanish, and all the work of trailing the man would have to be done over.

By evening he had straightened up the lower camp well enough that someone else could take it in charge, and he decided to whip back to Manitou when Strap went. With Flood so scared, so certain to take some drastic step, these hours were critical. He had pushed Flood into a bad psychological corner and ought to keep the man there. If he stayed here he would be allowing humane considerations to ball him up, precisely as when he had flung that short-fused dynamite into Frank Rocco's hangout.

Near seven o'clock Thomkins came down with word that Harla wished to see him. Thinking that she might be laying some plan to get back to Manitou herself, he knocked off work and walked up to the stone cross, where Strap was cooking supper for himself and Thomkins and Brannigan.

"She's over yon," Strap informed, jerking a thumb toward the canoe landing. "Tea for two, you lucky devil. Us plain bozos don't rate. Scram, or I'll throw some soup on you."

Wondering what Strap meant, Noel walked across to the river bank and found Harla waiting there. At the edge of a pine clump she had spread a supper for herself and him, on the carpet of needles. She had prepared the meal herself and had gone to considerable trouble to make it nice, laying a blanket for table-cloth and even gathering a cluster of Arctic poppies.

If he could possibly have done it, Noel would have excused himself and got away from there. All day he had studiously avoided Harla, on the principle of "out of sight, out of mind." And now, this supper with her, a half-hour ordeal—and short of wounding her unthinkably, he would have to go through with it.

They sat down, and Harla poured tea for him. He knew that this would be their last meal together, and he forced himself to be friendly, in the old way. She seemed pathetically eager to make atonement for the past fortnight. Again and again he caught her looking at him oddly, across the poppy bouquet, as though she sensed his change toward her and was badly cut up by it.

"Why I wanted to see you alone, Noel," she said, seeking excuse for the privacy of this supper for two, "I found out something awf'ly important this afternoon. It's about this contagion—how it ever struck this isolated band. Besides those mountain barriers, this basin and a big block of surrounding territory is the Dinokui Preserve. It's rigidly barred against whites and *métis* and alien Indians. The Indian Bureau had it made *défendu* by an Order-in-Council."

"What! *Défendu?*" Noel echoed, astonished. On the *Midnight Sun* he had heard about the Yellow-knife and Thelon limits but not one word about any preserve within striking distance of Manitou. "Are you sure about this?"

"I ought to be; I helped draw up those papers for the Bureau. But about this news of mine. I heard it from one of these Dinokui women, through Tah-Gomaugh. About twenty days ago several Dinokui families were camped at a fish weir fifteen miles up river. One twilight a white man and a Dog-rib 'breed appeared at their camp. The 'breed was very sick; he lay in the canoe on a bear rug and didn't help paddle; and his companion had to carry him ashore. They ate a meal with the Dinokuis, traded a few articles, then skirled away, northwest."

"Hmmph. That looks like the explanation of this outbreak, all right."

"The Mounted ought to run those men down, Noel. They're a walking menace in this country. Who d'you suppose they are?"

"I can't imagine," Noel said, little interested in that pair of obscure bush-lopers. His thoughts had gone racing off at a different tangent. Forbidden territory, rigidly barred ... Mere trespassing in a *défendu* region carried a six-month penalty. Trapping or prospecting thereon carried a heavy penitentiary sentence.

"Lord," he breathed to himself, "maybe Jimmy's placer is on this Dinokui Preserve! If it is, why, there's the reason he didn't stake and file, or go to the Mounted for protection, or tell a soul about his discovery! And maybe there's the explanation of what he said to me in Winnipeg, that his job was technically illegal but it didn't harm a person on earth."

"What's the matter?" Harla asked, noticing his queer silence.

"Nothing at all," he denied casually, judging it wise to tell her nothing. Her work with the Dinokui women had drawn her thoughts away from Flood and Jimmy, and he did not care even to mention their names to her.

Though he jumped to no conclusion, he was all but certain now that Jimmy's secret was really a placer and that it was located somewhere in these wild Silvertips. If he could get some clue to its location, from Tah-Gomaugh or the Dinokui men, then he would have a throttle-hold on Flood, and the man could not possibly slip him. Flood was after that rich prize. He had murdered Jimmy to get it. Very likely he needed it as money backing for his other unknown and criminal enterprises. Soon or late he would show up, at that placer, and there he could be nailed.

"Strap told me that you're returning to Manitou with him this evening," Harla remarked, when they had finished supper and were walking back to the stone cross.

"I've got a job or two yet to do here," Noel answered enigmatically. "I'm staying. This country and this trip are considerably more, ah, interesting than I'd imagined."

He hurried back to the *kozgee* camp and plunged into work again, impatient to get after his investigation.

A little before sun-down Strap and Thomkins lifted the Bellanca out of the river and circled above the village, climbing higher and higher till the plane was a glistening red speck and its motor song was as faint as a mosquito's hum. At fifteen thousand feet the ship lined away for the Mackenzie and vanished behind the mountains.

After supervising another meal, Noel built a circle of smudges against the mosquitoes and *brûlés,* gave a round of medicine to his patients, and kindled a large bright fire, under the pines, for his little group. They had no need of its warmth, but a fire would cheer them up and drive away the dark specters of their fevered imaginations.

By the time he had got his "pine ward" ready for the night, it was eleven o'clock. The sun had dipped below the northwestern ranges, and the Dinokui basin was filling with deep purple shadows. Through the mantling twilight he started for the upper camp, to have a talk with Tah-Gomaugh.

He was so tired and sleepy that he felt like chucking everything and crawling into one of those cooking pits for a bit of rest; but this *défendu* news was a hot trail, and he was keen to run it. If any of these Indians could give him a clue to Jimmy's placer, Tah-Gomaugh was the person. An iconoclastic young fellow, scornful of the magic and superstition of his people, Tah-Gomaugh was alert and open-eyed. Besides, he had been in to Manitou quite a lot, and there was a chance, even, that he had hooked up with Jimmy as guide or bush-partner.

At the upper edge of the cross he came upon Constable Brannigan, sitting on a ritual stone, smoking, slapping at mosquitoes.

"Where's Tah-Gomaugh, Brannigan?"

"U'nt know," Brannigan grunted, peevish and out of sorts. Whether angry at taking orders from a woman or resentful because his authority had been usurped, he had sulked all day, scarcely turning a hand.

"Where's Miss Harla, then?"

"U'nt know. I'm not toddling around at her heels."

"Where did you last see her?"

"Over in them pines a while ago, getting some smudge stuff."

His surliness angered Noel. "Why didn't you get that stuff yourself instead of making a tired girl do it, Big Chief Sit-and-Smoke? And talking about sitting, is that ritual stone the only place you could find to plunk yourself down on? D'you want these people here mad at us?"

"Hell, who's afraid of a bunch of Smokies, and sick 'uns at that?"

"You miserable excuse," Noel said, in weary disgust, "you must have got into the Mounted Police by climbing a fence."

He walked across to the river-bank pines, called for Harla; came back to the upper camp and looked around for her among the scattered stone dwellings. At a small fire near the north wall he finally found Tah-Gomaugh, comfortably fixed up for the night.

"Tah-Gomaugh, where's Miss Harla?"

"She gone, huh?"

"Seems to be, I can't find her anywhere."

"She mebbe sleep. Mebbe take sleep-poke, find quiet place. She bad tired. She say, 'Tah-Gomaugh, I could drop.'"

So tired himself that he ached, Noel could appreciate the remark. Undoubtedly, as Tah-Gomaugh thought, Harla had taken her blanket roll to some secluded nook and was catching an hour or two of badly needed sleep.

He lit a pipe and sat down on a rock beside Tah-Gomaugh and struck up a friendly talk.

The gibbous moon had brightened into silver; the twilight had come on; a midnight hush lay over the old stone town. From the burial islets and the woods across the river floated the macaber hooting of owls. The night was so still that for twenty miles back in the mountains he could hear the crescendo wailing of solitary dog wolves, ranging alone while their mates of the spring moons were leading their half-grown cubs to rabbit thickets and lemming slopes.

With a few deft questions he found out that Tah-Gomaugh had met Jimmy once or twice at Manitou but had not been associated with the youngster in any way.

He led the talk around, then, to the subject of gold; and there again he drew a complete blank. The Dinokuis had no interest in gold or any metal except silver, and in that only as something to make squaw gewgaws of. Strictly a stone-culture people, their idea of a rich mineral strike was a good flint quarry or a lense of black obsidian.

Disappointed, Noel switched the talk to airplanes. Had Tah-Gomaugh ever seen any plane within the Dinokui range? Or heard of any?

With unexpected suddenness this last question struck solid gold ore—a story about a plane.

Tah-Gomaugh himself had not seen the ship. He merely repeated the account of his older brother, of whom Tah-Gomaugh seemed to have a very poor opinion indeed. "He talk wild, like Waa-haaaaa-hoo, the red loon," Tah-Gomaugh scoffed. "He believe all these old-squaw stories 'bout magic and Familiars; he never been 'cross mountains to Big River; he don't know nothing. Uh, *he* saw plane, all right! Listen. You laugh hard."

With a grin on his swart young face, Tah-Gomaugh repeated the wild-eyed story which his brother had told him, two moons ago. Early that summer, during the Moon-of-No-Nights, this brother and another youngster went hunting bighorns in the headwaters country northwest of the Dinokui basin. One day when they were walking along the shore of a moraine lake, a great red-and-black creature, in form like the mosquito-wolf or dragonfly but with a body bigger than a canoe and with the wing-spread of five eagles, flapped out from behind a mountain and swooped down at them like a hungry hawk upon a lemming, with a bellowing voice louder than a thunder-roll.

Only by quick work, by leaping for a pile of avalanche débris and squirming back among the dank logs and rocks, did they save themselves from being seized and eaten.

Baffled and so angry that it spat fire, the huge creature cunningly lit at the upper end of the lake and hid itself behind a willow islet, waiting for them to venture out.

But they were too wise for that. For six whole rounds of the sun they stayed back in that dark cold tangle, till the great bird-beast finally got tired of waiting and flew away, over the eastern mountains.

"And they said," Tah-Gomaugh chuckled feebly, "that it flap wings, spit fire, bellow, try to eat them up!" He laughed at the thought of how his imaginative brother had shivered in that cold débris for nearly a week, afraid of a mere airplane. "You ever hear crazier story as that, huh?"

Noel managed to laugh heartily, and agreed that the incident was a great joke on this stupid brother. But within himself he did not laugh. The story was too portentous. That red-and-black bird-beast was nothing more or less than Jimmy DeLong's red-and-black Diomede. And that moraine lake, or its immediate vicinity, held Jimmy's secret, the rich placer.

With a dead pipe in his teeth, he gazed thoughtfully into the northwest, at those dark and forbidding headwater mountains. Up yonder, thirty miles distant, lay Jimmy's fatal prize. Only thirty miles—and he had come three thousand on this hunt! Step by step, through good luck and bad, he had steadily closed in till now he could lift his eyes and see the end of his long trail.

"Richer than Fraser's Cradle in the Golden Caribou"—that's what Jimmy had said. What sort of place was it? A pocket in some dark canyon? A dried-up lake, ages old? Or some geological prank played by the mountain gods who had built these Silvertips so helter-skelter?

He wanted to go up there and have a look at that mysterious prize, but the dark mystery surrounding Raphael Flood lured him even more. Back to Manitou, keeping himself alive, boring into Flood and his unknown background, yanking the man and his career out of the shadows into the light of day—that was his job and his line of thrust now.

CHAPTER FOURTEEN

T HROUGH the one o'clock dawn, while he worked with several desperately ill patients, he kept watching the upper camp for Harla.

At sun-rise he dropped his work and went up there, sharply uneasy.

One glance told him that she had not been around since last twilight. Her smudges had all gone out, and the big campfire which she too had built to cheer her patients had burned to ashes. Restless and leaderless, the Dinokui women were looking for her and wondering where she had disappeared.

At a cooking pit Constable Brannigan was getting breakfast for himself—pancakes, bacon, coffee, canned fruit, marmalade, toast.

"Have you seen anything of Miss Harla since daybreak?" Noel asked him.

"Ain't bothered to look."

"Why in hell," Noel demanded, in hot anger, "didn't you keep these fires going and watch after this camp? And how can you squat there cooking breakfast for your own healthy self when here's a bunch of sick women and kids needing food and care?"

"I'm not flunkeying for any Smokies. I'm a Mounted, fellow, and don't you forget that."

"A Mounted—you? Why, you miserable hunk of nothing, you're not decent bait for a Mounted Police dog team."

He went on, found Tah-Gomaugh awake, bade him tell the Dinokui women to look in all the stone houses for Harla and search the whole upper camp.

He himself hurried over to the river-edge pines, thinking that Harla might have spread her blanket roll in the quiet of that drogue. She was not there.

When he came back, Tah-Gomaugh reported that she was nowhere within the upper village.

"Squaws look everywhere, call aloud, poke into every place. She gone."

A cold fear seized Noel. Something had happened to Harla, in the twilight of last evening. Where was she? What was the nature of this oblivion which had reached out and touched her?

There was a chance, one in a hundred, that she had outwitted him and slipped back to Manitou, to settle her score with Flood. She might have connived with Strap or even stowed away on the big Bellanca.

"When and where did *you* last see her?" he asked Tah-Gomaugh.

The young Indian thought for a moment. "Last time was up by that wall, when she fix my fire, fix me for sleep."

"Was this *before* or *after* the plane left?"

"After. While red plane circle over island, she straighten up from giving me pill and drink, and wave hank'chief at Strap man."

This flat-out statement, exploding any possibility that Harla had returned to Manitou, fairly dazed Noel. For a little space he leaned weakly against the stone wall, with something near to panic gripping him. The avalanche which he had expected and dreaded for days had at last piled down, and it was Harla who had been caught in the slideway.

The nature of her vanishing was as clear to him as if he had seen the incident with his own eyes. Since disposing of Jimmy, Flood had established a camp up yonder at that placer. Yesterday a canoe party of his men had dropped down the Dinokui River and scouted out this village. In the owl-dusk of last evening they had landed on this island and watched for a clean chance to seize Harla. When she went over among those dark pines for the smudge stuff, she had walked squarely into their hands.

Fighting against this dread guess, he hurried back to the *kozgee* camp and ordered eight of the Dinokui men to comb the entire island, look for Harla, look carefully for any suspicious tracks or signs.

While they were doing this, he himself tried to work, but the work dropped from his hands, and he stood by the *kozgee* door, looking up across the island, praying to see Harla appear yonder among the rocks and pines. But he knew, in his heart, that somewhere on the upper Dinokui she was lying bound in a canoe that was headed for Flood's main camp.

It seemed unbelievable that Flood would venture so brazen a move at so critical a time. Didn't the man realize that Harla DeLong was a person of some importance and that her disappearance would not go unnoticed? Didn't he know that the crime would surely be charged to him? That his act would rouse the agencies of the law like a rock through a hornet nest? When he had been panicky already, why had he laid himself wide open, like this, to destruction?

The man's lawless nature and his infatuation for Harla did not quite explain his move. Flood was no fool, no gambler, but a coward who played safe, always. He had captured Harla for some reason connected with his own safety.

Within ten minutes one of the Dinokui men came hurrying toward the *kozgee*. Noel went to meet him. The Indian took him up to the pine drogue, into the pines; began pointing here and there on the needle carpet and talking excitedly.

Noel could not understand a word of the talk; and of the rapid gestures he understood only one, repeated many times: four fingers—four men in that party. To his eyes that needle carpet was a blank; he saw no tracks, no signs. But to the Indian's eyes … With unerring precision the man led him on and on, through a thicket of deerbush, around a clump of thorny devil's-club, to the bank of the river; and there, under a broad-sweeping old pine that overhung the water, the Dinokui pointed out a sign which Noel did see and understand. In the silty gravel, the marks of a sharp-keeled canoe. One mark where the craft had been grounded and lifted back into the shadows. Another mark where the canoe had been slid to water again.

For several minutes he stood there by the pine, looking at those far blue mountains and trying to shake off his daze. Flood's move had neatly spiked all his plans. He could not return to Manitou now and abandon Harla. He could not push his hunt against Flood; in fact, he dared not raise a hand against the man. Flood was holding a fearful club over him now—Harla's safety.

"Why, hell," he breathed, "there it is! He grabbed her in order to stop me! He was out-and-out panicky. He's going to use her as his guarantee of immunity. As long as he's got her he's safe, and he knows it. If I can't get her away from him, I'm done, I'm washed up."

He knew that Flood would not keep her at that headwaters camp but would whisk her away to some distant and secure hiding place. Just where he would take her—that question was as huge as this huge North. In that swift gray plane he could take her anywhere, to any of his secret camps—anywhere in the two-thousand-mile length and breadth of the Three Rivers country.

With a swift estimate of time and distance, he saw that he stood a good chance to free her if he worked fast. Flood's canoe party had not yet reached the moraine lake. The trip was thirty miles, up-stream miles. A four-paddle canoe would be ten or twelve hours making that trip. A plane could make it in twenty minutes.

To splash Flood's outfit he would need help, rifle help. That was coming, this Police detail—due at any time now. With two planes and half a dozen seasoned men he could fly up there, land on that camp unexpectedly and clean it out.

He hated to break this case open precipitantly, before he was fully armed with knowledge of Flood's background. Above all, he hated to run any risk of killing Flood. If Flood should die in a rifle battle, with his past unknown and his crimes unrevealed, he too might be apotheosized, like Frank Rocco, by that million-headed but thoughtless "man in the street."

But if he failed to lead a party up there, he would be betraying Harla. It was he who had brought her into these mountains, and therefore he was responsible for her. An innocent girl, caught in this pitiless battle between Flood and himself, she had suffered tragedy enough already.

It was high noon, that day, before the Mounted detail came.

As Noel worked at the *kozgee* camp, he heard the faint singing whine of two airplanes in the southeastern sky. A minute later Strap's red Bellanca, followed by a large cabined biplane, swam in between two towering pinnacles and started the long glide into the basin.

On raw edge after his all-morning wait, Noel hurried up the river bank. The planes were hours over-due, hours later than he had reckoned on. By this time Flood's canoe party likely had reached the moraine lake.

The Bellanca spiraled down, alighted on the river and glided into the shallows. Without stopping the motor, Strap climbed down upon a float, ordered Thomkins to turn the plane around for an immediate take-off, and came wading ashore, a letter in his hand.

"What's hit you, fellow?" Strap greeted. "You look sick."

Noel did not answer. He pointed at the letter. "That's for me, isn't it?"

"Why, how the devil did you know? Yes, it is. A bloke at Manitou—never saw the cuss before—gave it to me and said to hand it to you the minute I landed here. He talked like it was important. Better read it."

Noel took the letter. "Why're you swinging that Bellanca, Strap?"

"Got to hop back to the River on the *hiyu* quick and get down to Aklavik. They're prodding me, down there. I'm under commission on that job, y' know."

As Noel slit the envelope of the letter, the biplane came taxiing into the shallows. He paid no attention to it or to the men preparing to disembark. Frowning in bewilderment, he stared at the single sheet of paper which he had pulled from the envelope.

The note was twelve short lines of neatly printed characters. The lines were not divided into words; the sequence of letters made no sense; the note appeared a meaningless jumble.

"Must be some sort of code," he thought. And then he saw that it was written in the "F-R" code which he and Spencer and the ranking eight of the Intelligence had used during the past year.

With a pencil stub and the back of the envelope, he broke the cipher down and wrote out the message.

Her safety depends on what you do, and *I'll* be the judge. Don't lay her disappearance to me. Explain her disappearance any way you see fit.

At McMurray, on your way out of the North, find letter of further instructions. Follow them, and no harm will come to her.

Noel read the note a second time, then tore the envelope to bits. The message, which he had expected, which he had *known* was coming, told him little that he did not know already. He had interpreted Flood's move correctly. The man had seized Harla to make him drop the hunt and get out of the North altogether.

To Flood's pledge of safety for Harla he pinned no more faith than he had ever pinned to promises from such men as Flood. The man intended only to shake off a menace, not to release

Harla. As a matter of fact the man did not dare release her. After he had exploited that rich placer and faded entirely out of the Dominion—if that was his intention—she might be released then. That would be months. Perhaps a whole year.

Strap broke into his thoughts. "I've seen people pull some weird boners, but you, Noel, you've pulled the prize boner of all my born days." He glanced at Constable Brannigan, who had just finished a good dinner and was sauntering down to meet the Mounted detail. "What a pretty kittle of fish you've cooked up, here! And *you* did it, you yourself."

"What did I do?"

"That wireless you sent to Inspector Clevenger—in Brannigan's name! The way you organized our party at Manitou and whipped in here to straighten up this camp and keep those men from pitching off—in Brannigan's name. Clevenger didn't know—six hundred miles away... He thinks Brannigan did all that. He gave Brannigan the credit for that live-wire piece of work."

"Who gives a damn about the credit? I used Brannigan's name to get action out of the Mounted."

"You did get action—and how! Clevenger thought, and I don't blame him, that anybody who started a job so splendelegantly, ought to finish it. So, believe it or not, but"—he gestured at Brannigan again—"that balky jackass there, picking his teeth, that hunk of lazy mud, that hairy-necked Missing Link, that ambulating Mistake, that walking-talking Vegetable, *he's* the boss of this detail and in charge of the whole cussed works here!"

"*What?* Brannigan, in charge here? You're crazy!"

"I'm telling you! He is And it's all your doings. He'll not only bungle this job but he'll sure ride you plenty, after the lip-larrupings you gave him yesterday. He loves you and Harla both."

Noel went pale. Brannigan, in charge here—the idea was so preposterous that he had laughed when Strap first broke the news. But the laugh died in his throat. The possible consequences of Clevenger's mistake were beginning to dawn on him, and he was frightened. Brannigan, who had exchanged some words with the Mounted detail, came sauntering up the land-wash, an exultant grin on his face.

"My God," Strap groaned, "he's so dumb, Noel, that he doesn't kumtux why he's boss here! He thinks he rates it."

Brannigan came up and planted himself wide-legged in front of Noel, and his grin changed to a vengeful leer.

"So I got into the Mounted P'lice by climbing a fence, hey? And I ain't decent bait for a P'lice dog team, hey? I'll fix you plenty for them remarks."

"And I'll fix you plenty with Clevenger, you engine knock!" Strap promised him hotly. "The first time I get to Fort James, I'll light a basket of firecrackers under you."

Brannigan doubled up his fists. "Keep your gib outa this. Get into that plane of your'n and get gone, like you're s'posed to, or I'll pinch you."

As Noel listened to their quarrel, his heart sank and his last-ditch plan of whipping up to those mountains and freeing Harla slowly crumbled away. Brannigan would never let him have this Mounted detail. In the blind way of an ignoramus, Brannigan was vengeful against him and Harla both, and by a crazy hapchance the stupid dolt was holding the whip-hand now. What use to tell *him* about Harla's plight? The unimaginative block-head would sneer at the story as a cock-and-bull yarn.

Even if the facts could be hammered into him, it would be a fool's act to tell him anything at all about Harla or Flood. Brannigan, operating against a man of Flood's power and brains—it was ridiculous and worse. One mistake, one wrong move, would have tragic consequences for Harla.

In this whole sorry crack-up of his plans, only one advantage remained with him: he could keep silent and keep this hunt in his own hands. And that he swore to do. If necessary he could say that Harla had stowed away on the Bellanca and gone back to the Mackenzie. Brannigan might bungle everything else but he was not going to bungle this case or endanger Harla's life by some half-baked and blundering attack against Flood.

Thinking swiftly, he decided to whip back to the River with Strap and organize a party to go after Harla. He would be free to act as he saw fit, and he would lead the party himself. If he could land on that camp within a few hours, Harla might still be there.

"Let's be getting gone," he said to Strap. "I'm going across to Manitou with you."

Brannigan stepped in front of him. "Yeah? So you're going to Manitou, are you?" He turned his head and looked down the landwash at the Mounted detail—four constables, a corporal and a government doctor. "Hey, Schuler," he called to the non-com, "this fellow says he's going to Manitou. Ain't that a good 'un!"

The corporal, a thin leathery-faced man of forty, started up the landwash.

"Who's he?" Noel asked Strap.

"Corporal Schuler, from New Northumbria—and the sourest pickle on the Three Rivers. Don't ruffle his feathers, Noel, whatever he wants with you. He's an old-timer, and so damn tough the mosquitoes can't bite him!"

With a premonition that some new calamity was about to fall, Noel watched Schuler draw near. A waspish individual, hardened by his two decades in the North and embittered at spending twenty years getting his two-stripes, the corporal seemed to be the "sour-pickle" that Strap had dubbed him; and just now his temper, never very genial, was not at all improved by the fact that a raw recruit from the Awkward Squad had been put in command here over his head.

In tones like a drill-sergeant's bark he demanded of Noel, "Your name Lanier?"

"Yes."

"Y'under arrest! I-warn-you-that-anything-you-say-will-be-used-against-you." He unbuttoned his shirt pocket and produced a warrant. "You flew an unlicensed airplane. Got no pilot's license. No prospector's license——"

"Oh hell," Strap put in, disgustedly, "he spit in the Mackenzie River without a license! Why don't you pinch him for saving these Dinokuis and stopping a bad spread, without a license?"

"Keep your lip to yourself," Schuler snapped at him. "Clear out for Aklavik." He swung on Noel again. "Now look—I'm giving you a little warning. I'm personally responsible for you. Clevenger ordered me to bring you to Fort James. He wants to give you a looking-over himself. Wants to know who you really are and what you're doing in this country. So I'm gluing onto you. You walk straight and I'll treat you decent, but one funny move and you'll find yourself hogtied."

Of themselves the charges and the arrest had no effect on Noel. When Clevenger found out who he was, those charges would be dropped like hot bricks. But in the meantime, the delay, a week, perhaps two weeks, in the tight custody of this sour corporal—that was what maddened him.

He realized that this arrest was Flood's handiwork. Through an anonymous wireless message, Flood had directed these charges and this suspicion at him. Wanting time to whisk Harla away and build up his crumbling defenses, the man had not relied upon his warning letter but had made assurance doubly sure by this skillfully maneuvered arrest.

Schuler took him by the arm. "C'mon. Up into the camp. Don't want you making any break for that Bellanca. I'd have to plunk you."

Noel shook off his hand and pushed him away. "Let me alone, you half-pint. I'm going back to Manitou. *I* came in here and straightened this camp up, while that jackass there sat on a rock and sulked; and now he's put in charge and I get arrested. To hell with you and your warrant."

Schuler grabbed him again. Noel's self-control snapped. He was scarcely himself and hardly realized what he was doing.

Two sleepless nights, all the heavy work and worry of this camp, the disaster to Harla, the crack-up of his plans, the insufferable Brannigan crowing over him, and now this crazy arrest on top of everything, dynamiting his last hope of freeing Harla—he was goaded beyond human endurance.

He wrenched loose from Schuler a second time, gave the corporal a push and sent him staggering backwards. As Schuler stumbled and fell, Brannigan jumped in and swung a clumsy blow at Noel's face. In a fury Noel smashed him on the jaw, rocked him with a quick one-two to the stomach, then drove in a swinging crash to Brannigan's chin that dropped the constable in his tracks.

"Let's scram!" Strap cried. "Come on, Noel—my Bellank!"

They whirled around—and ran squarely into two of the Mounted constables.

"Not so fast," one of them suggested, and he emphasized the order with a flip of his rifle barrel. "Go on and clear out, Barclay. You can't whip a warrant. Let's not have trouble."

Schuler got up and brushed his clothes. One of the constables helped Brannigan to his feet. With tears of rage in his eyes Strap was glaring at that rifle muzzle.

"If you're through kicking and prancing, let's go," Schuler ordered Noel. "I may be a half-pint, but I can tie good knots."

Noel gave in. Against six rifle-armed men, there was nothing else to do. With Schuler gripping his arm, he started up the stone walk toward the cross.

His helplessness maddened him, but he was too weary to plead or argue and too dazed to think clearly. A prisoner, under arrest; the precious hours fleeting; Harla in Flood's power—it was more like a nightmare than sober reality.

As he trudged up the path, hopeless and sick at heart, he kept his eyes on the black stones underfoot, to shut out the sight of those blue mountains yonder.

CHAPTER FIFTEEN

I N the small stone hut where he had been jailed since noon, Noel was lying quiet in his blankets, impatiently waiting for the dark to tighten down a little more.

As though taking his automatic, jailing him and tying him up, hand and foot, was not security enough, Corporal Schuler had asked Brannigan to sit guard over him during the two hours of twilight, knowing that the vengeful constable would do a good sentry job.

By clenching an obsidian chip in his teeth and sawing his wrist-bands across the knife-sharp edge of it, Noel had cut himself loose, half an hour ago. The next step in his getaway was to handle Brannigan, sitting just outside the door. After Brannigan, he would have to slip out of the hut and fade without being seen by the two constables who were smoking and talking at a bright fire thirty feet distant.

He believed he could get free all right, but what he was going to do with that freedom he did not precisely know. The trail ahead was a suicide trail, if he ever had seen one. Alone in a savage country, without plane or outfit, probably without even a weapon, he would be pitting himself against Flood's whole party. At bush-work, such as faced him, one man like young Paul d'Orleans was worth half a dozen of himself. And Flood must have ten or twelve superlative men up yonder at the placer camp.

Beyond the intention of getting up there and doing whatever he could for Harla, he had no plans at all. There was a chance, a gambler's chance, that Harla would still be there. If so, he might be able to pry her free and then cover her back trail while she escaped.

If he got rubbed out, the main purpose of his hunt would flow along just the same. In a fortnight Herm Spencer would be slipping in to Manitou, backed up by the picked men who had helped corner and kill Frank Rocco. Flood would undoubtedly relax caution, with his chief enemy out of the picture; and Spencer would take him.

As he lay there in the dark, wishing or hoping for little except Harla's safety, the conviction rested upon him that he was not to come out of those mountains alive. And such was his mood that he hardly cared the turn of his hand. He was alone in life; his Mounted career had cracked up; he had no money or profession or anything but a cruelly unjust disgrace to show for the best years of his manhood. And he could think of Harla only with pain and a great emptiness at heart.

He fully intended, if he got half a chance, to break open a fight with Flood's men and smear that outfit up all he could, whether it cost him his life or not. With no martyrdom about it but with a good deal of vengeance, he swore that those people who had talked so much about Frank Rocco's "gallant death" were going to see what the genuine article looked like ....

In the darkness of the hut he slipped out of his blankets, stood up noiselessly and moved over beside the door, gripping a little blackjack which he had braided from Schuler's manila rope.

From where he stood he could have reached out and slugged Brannigan, but he doubted whether he could knock the man out cleanly enough. The slightest commotion would draw attention from those constables at the fire.

Standing tight against the wall, he made a slight scratchy noise on a stone, with his fingernail. As he expected, Brannigan turned around, snapped on his flashlight and pointed it through the doorway.

"What'n hell!" Brannigan exclaimed beneath his breath, as the yellow shaft played on the empty blankets.

Instead of sensing danger and speaking to the constables before investigating, he came blundering inside and began poking the light at the dark corners of the hut.

Tensed and ready, Noel swung at him with the crude blackjack and smashed him across the forehead. Dropping the blackjack, he sprang on Brannigan and clapped a hand over his mouth to keep him from making any outcry.

But Brannigan did not even grunt. Knocked completely senseless, the constable sagged and went limp on him, so limp that Noel had to ease him to the stone floor.

Kneeling down, he made a quick practiced search of the man's clothes, took his big jackknife, his "issue" compass and match-case.

In Brannigan's tunic pocket, he found an automatic. The weapon felt oddly familiar. As he held it to the light, a little tingle of joy went through him. His own automatic! The gun which he had carried for nearly a decade, on his dangerous jobs, his close brushes with death. Brannigan had evidently taken a fancy to the weapon and stolen it from Schuler.

"You hulking coward," Noel thought, gratefully dropping the automatic into his own pocket, "if you knew of all the places where that gun has been, you'd be scared to touch it!"

He carried Brannigan across to the blanket roll, bound and gagged him, and slipped him into the blankets. Then he groped around on the floor till he found three small fragments of stone, and stepped over to the door again.

Selecting the lightest of the three fragments, he drew back his arm and threw the stone out into the darkness, over the heads of the constables.

As the rock landed, some forty feet beyond the two, they stopped talking and turned around, trying to see what had made the noise.

Noel flung a second stone. At its clatter on the gravel, the two men stood up and peered sharply into the semi-dark.

"What d'you reckon?" one demanded.

"Don't know. If it's one of these sick Smokies wandering loose, we'd better catch him and take him back to Doc Morrisey."

They picked up their rifles and started in the direction of the noise. Dropping his third rock, Noel eased through the door, glided around the hut into the darkness behind it, and headed for the drogue of trees ....

As he hurried past the clump of devil's-club and drew near the old patriarchal pine by the river bank, a dark silent figure emerged from the landwash willows. Noel stepped up.

"Good Tah-Gomaugh!" he whispered, hastily. "I knew I could count on you. How about the canoe—were you able to get one for me?"

The young Indian pointed at a dainty ten-foot birch-bark half awash in the black pine shadows.

"There! Good canoe. Mine. Easy tote on portage; swift as brown otter in water."

"Fine. Thanks, Tah-Gomaugh. And the other things we talked about this afternoon—did you get any of them?"

"Got grub, plenty grub. Dry caribou, dry goat. But no shoulder gun." He swayed weakly and caught Noel's arm to steady himself. "No chance to steal shoulder gun."

"That's all right; I've got a hand gun; I'll make out. How about that map of the upper Dinokui and the lake?"

Tah-Gomaugh handed him a little scroll of birch paper. "There map."

"Heavens! While I was asking you for things, Tah-Gomaugh, I should have asked for an airplane and some bombs. I believe, on my word, you'd have produced 'em!"

He pushed the canoe afloat and stood holding it by the curled prow while he gave Tah-Gomaugh some last instructions. Reluctantly, that afternoon, he had taken the young Indian into his confidence, under the pressure of necessity; and he saw now that he had made no mistake. This boy, from a primitive and benighted people, possessed the priceless quality of trustworthiness in a way that put most white men to shame.

"One word more, Tah-Gomaugh," he said. "And this word is the most important of all that I have told you. Listen carefully.

"As soon as you are well enough to make the trip, go in to Manitou post. Wait there. Within this next moon a man will come, a friend to me." In swift detail he described Herm Spencer. "You go to that man, Tah-Gomaugh, and give him this ring of mine as a sign that you are my messenger. Then tell him how these men stole Miss Harla. Tell him about their camp and the placer. Tell him everything that I have said to you. Will you do this, now?"

Tah-Gomaugh nodded. But his eyes were upon those dark headwater mountains, and he was loath for his white friend to leave.

"No good you go up there, 'lone, one man fighting *hyas* men," he said. "You will *float* back down Dinokui River, and not in canoe, either."

The prophecy sent a shiver through Noel. His own fear, his own premonition—Tah-Gomaugh had put it into words.

"Let me go 'long," Tah-Gomaugh pleaded. "Harla woman help save my people. I want help save her."

Noel had seldom seen sheer fortitude like that. To pay an honor debt this young Indian, half dead on his feet, was begging part in a hard wilderness trip and asking to share that gamble of "floating back down" the Dinokui.

"No, Tah-Gomaugh," he refused firmly. "You must go in to Manitou with that ring and my message. If you do that, you will really be helping Miss Harla. Besides, you are too sick to go with me. On the portages I would have to carry you like a papoose. You have driven yourself too long now. You must go back to the *kozgee* camp, Tah-Gomaugh, and let the white medico take good care of you."

With a handshake and a final word of thanks, he shoved the canoe afloat, stepped in, skirled out upon the twilight Dinokui and headed north.

Around ten o'clock of the next evening, while the sun was slanting down toward the northwestern peakline and the first hush of twilight was stealing into the wilderness valley, Noel made a last portage, up along a quarter-mile of plunging white waters; and came out to the edge of the moraine lake where that huge bird-beast once had tried to gobble up Tah-Gomaugh's older brother.

The high watershed country into which he had penetrated was unwordably raw and bleak. Since leaving the lush sheltered basin at noon that day, he had climbed with the dwindling Dinokui River all afternoon and evening, past tumultuous rapids and bridal-veil overfalls, steadily higher and higher, till here at trail-end he found himself in a wild cloudland region of bare granite and icy waters, where the gods of summer and of winter seemed to be fighting a deadlocked battle for mastery.

He saw no birds, no flowers; there was no lichen to soften the rocks, no wolf-foot to carpet the ground. The scrubby banksians, stunted and warped by the harsh struggle for existence, were storm-gnarled caricatures of trees; and the cold wind flowing down valley like a tangible stream brought him a chill freezing breath from fields of perpetual ice and snow.

Yet, in Noel's eyes, that bleak watershed country, that strange wild *haut d'en pays*, had a certain beauty of its own. Not the warm rich beauty of the basin, but a cold purity and an elemental grandeur. Against the glistening white of its *névés* the slant sun was shattering into a thousand fires, as from fields of diamond dust; and the wind that soughed through the pines with steady moan braced and challenged him for the work ahead.

A scattering of rocky islets kept him from seeing the upper end of the lake. He selected the tallest of the near-by banksians and climbed to its swaying top, where he had good view.

At his first sweeping glance his eyes hardened, and all the weariness of those thirty up-stream miles fell away from him. Near the upper shore of the lake, a thousand yards distant, two planes rode at anchor, on either side of a willow headland. One was Flood's yellow Albatross. The other was that ghost plane, the gray machine-gunned ship.

The unexpected sight of the gray plane still at this base camp set his heart pounding. Harla was up there. Not a thousand miles distant, at some unknown hiding place, but almost within call of him!

But then he checked back across the hours, and saw that there had been plenty of time, an entire day, for that swift plane to have carried her away and returned. She might not be there at all.

Parting the pine branches to see better, he looked up across the lake and islands and studied the layout. Two hundred yards above the far lake shore a seventy-foot cliff stretched across the valley. On top of that cliff and back in the pines was Flood's camp. The camp itself was out of sight, but a wisp of blue smoke was curling above the trees there. A supper fire. Flood's men were getting their evening meal.

He climbed down the pine, hid Tah-Gomaugh's canoe in some windfall, cut back into the buckbrush where he could not be seen, and started for the upper end of the lake.

A feverish haste burned in him, and he hurried. Before the dark came on, he wanted a look at Jimmy's rich placer, the secret which had lured and baffled him across three thousand miles. And if Harla was still there at that camp, he would have to plan his strike, pry her free and see that she got a good headstart down the Dinokui. All this during one brief hour of dark.

As he made his way through the buckbrush, he wondered how Flood had first got wind of this mining prize, here in these

wild sub-Arctic Rockies. Edmonton looked like the answer to
that. Jimmy must have made occasional flights outside and disposed of his dust. To escape the heavy royalty duty and avoid
explaining where he had got that gold, Jimmy had sold his dust to
under-cover agencies. Through those fly-by-nights, trafficking in
anonymous dust and wildcat promotions, Flood had heard that
a youth was periodically coming out of the North with a poke of
raw gold. The man had trailed Jimmy, put him on the spot and
eventually killed him.

That story was easy enough to reconstruct, but what was the
rest of Flood's background? Where had he sprung from? Who
was he? If this far-North adventure was merely an interlude with
him, what was his main sphere of crime?

And that Mounted code, in which Flood had written his
message of warning—where had the man got hold of that? Herm
Spencer, an expert with codes, had built that particular cipher a
year ago for a special use. Only eight other men on earth were
familiar with it, and those eight were men of unquestionable
integrity. Not even the Mounted higher-ups knew that code. But
Flood did! Somewhere, somehow, the man had bored into the
Intelligence and possessed himself of one of their tightest secrets.
The trick was not impossible, but it had been terrifically difficult.

Why had Flood gone to such great pains? The answer there
was very plain, very startling. During the past year Flood had
had some extremely urgent reason for wanting to know what the
Intelligence was doing!

All this meant that Flood had not been in South America or
anywhere abroad, but right in Canada and right up against the
Police. A master criminal standing back in the shadows, he had
gone unknown and unsuspected—till now.

A dozen times, on his lone trip up the Dinokui, Noel had
pieced together the various facts which he definitely knew about
Flood. Like the parts of a jigsaw, they fitted all right and they
made a clear picture. But that picture was so preposterous that

he had thrown it out. Repeatedly he had told himself: "You're tired, overstrained. You're imagining all sorts of crazy things." Repeatedly he had scrambled the parts of that puzzle and tried to force them into some different design. But with every attempt, out came that same preposterous picture. No other design would work. No other explanation fitted the hard facts.

He believed he knew, now, where Flood had come from and who the man was....

Near the upper end of the lake he came to a swath of avalanche débris which offered him a good hiding place. Wanting to study the lay of the land at close range, he crawled back among the dank logs and rocks and looked down through the gathering dusk.

Just a hundred yards down slope from him the headland jutted into the lake. In the willows at the point sat a stocky half-breed, a rifle in his lap, guarding the planes for the night.

From the headland a well-worn foot-path led up through a fissure in the cliff, and disappeared in the scraggly timber above. He still could not see the camp, but he heard a man singing and someone chopping wood.

Between the head of the lake and the foot of that old dolomite cliff lay Jimmy's placer.

It was a round sunken area of pea-gravel, red Jurassic clay and polished black boulders. As placers went, it was very small, a mere pocket scarcely a hundred yards across. Up near the bottom of the cliff Jimmy's little handmade trough flume and tom-rocker had been kicked aside, and Flood had recently installed a metal pipe flume and three shiny mechanical rockers, evidently brought in by plane.

A small torrent of icy glacial water plunged over the top of the cliff, dropped into a little caldron pool near the "workings" and wound down across the gravel to the lake.

For the first minute or two, as he looked at the placer and tried to figure it out, Noel felt keenly disappointed. He had expected to see something spectacular; and here, apparently, was nothing but an inconsequential bit of gravel and boulders. How could that little area down there be any sort of placer, let alone one with a concentration richer than Fraser's Cradle? When "pay dirt" was water-made, usually it took a good-sized stream to do the job; certainly a bigger stream than that small blue torrent yonder.

It was those stream-bed boulders which gave him the key to the riddle and set him to reconstructing the story of that placer— a tale centuries old and as fascinating as any human story he had ever pieced together. As he studied those boulders, water-worn and polished, he realized that they had been transported from some black formation far up valley. But, transported by what? That little torrent, even at its break-up height, could never budge those big rocks. At some epoch in the past a stream of good size and power must have flowed down this valley. Something had happened to that ancient stream. A gigantic talus slide or a volcanic upheaval or some mighty folding of rock strata had turned that stream into a new channel, and now nothing was left of it save the little torrent.

But in the heyday of that bygone river this whole sunken area of gravel, clay and boulders had been a huge caldron pool, where the stream came roaring over that seventy-foot overfalls. For long ages the waters of that vanished river had come down from rock and mineral lode back among those peaks, bringing float gold and wheat-grain nuggets, and had thundered down into that ancient caldron pool. That pool had been a trap, a huge "pan" or settling basin for the yellow metal. The gravel and clay had been swept on down, had replaced itself season after season; but the heavier gold had sunk, had stayed in the pool, had piled up concentration for untold centuries.

After a time he turned his gaze from the placer to the 'breed sentry in the willows, and tried to figure out some way of handling the man. If he could bag that *métis*, he would not only acquire a badly needed rifle and have one less enemy to deal with but would clear the road for Harla's escape.

To slip up close enough to slug the man, as he had slugged Brannigan, was flatly impossible to a cheechako like himself. He could not even work close enough to get the drop.

The *métis* seemed badly bored with his sentry job. From a piece of slippery willow, a foot long and thick as a corncob, he had made himself a "trombone whistle" and was practicing on it, giving an atrocious rendition of the *Three Fairy Ducks*. Someone had brought him his supper a short while ago: an empty tin plate, with knife and spoon, lay on one of the gas drums, and occasionally the *métis* stopped his musical efforts long enough to gulp some tea from a tin can beside him.

"Since I can't come to you," Noel thought, with an idea taking shape in his mind, "you'll have to come to me, Mahomet. And I think I know how to bring you."

He was not at all sure of his plan; but with a similar stratagem he and Herm Spencer, several years ago at Vancouver, had played upon a dope runner's temper and lured the man right up to the muzzles of their guns.

From a banksian windfall he plucked a little ribbon of inner bark, trimmed it thin and narrow with his knife, and put the sliver between his thumbs as children do with a blade of grass.

The first sliver did not work. He tried three more before getting one that exactly suited him . . . .

With his trombone whistle, Pierre Pokonto, the *métis* guard, was amusing himself most agreeably. A good supper inside of one, a pipe going well, a tin of sweetened tea at one's elbow, and this instrument of music wherewith one could play *chansons* to the heart's delight—what more could one ask of *le bon Dieu?*

But there had come about, in the last few minutes, a fly in the ointment; a fly most annoying and of increasing vexation to one who was discoursing music. Up the slope, in the *débris-là* of that avalanche, some squeaky little imp of Satan, some befurred little morsel of malevolence, was mocking at one. Whether it was a lemming or a rabbit-of-the-rock, one did not know; but whenever one began to render a *chanson,* it began to go *squink-squink-squink.* When one stopped, it stopped. When one started, it started. Therefore and *sans* doubt, it was making malicious mockery of one.

In disgust Pierre finally took the whistle from his lips. "Shut op, *squink!*" he barked at the débris where the annoyance was coming from. "*Cache* yourself. Outside wit' you."

He started the *Three Fairy Ducks* once more. Immediately began that shrill and irritating *squink-squink-squink.*

Pierre stopped. The noise stopped. By way of test, Pierre let out one single note. Back came one single *squink.* He let out two notes. Back came *squink-squink.*

Thoroughly exasperated, he laid his whistle aside, picked up a fist-sized rock and sent it clattering up into the débris.

"Dere, damn your leetle hide!" he rapped, brushing his hands. "Mebbe dat dry you op. One more *squink,* and I shoot de geezzard out of you!"

Quite certain that the clattering rock had sent that befurred irritation skittering into its hole, he sat down, took a swig of tea, reached for his whistle and began on *Little White Wolf of the Sea.*

At his very first note that diabolic *squink-squink-squink* started up again. With a snort of anger Pierre swung around, so hastily that his arm knocked the tin of tea from the rock. Enraged at the loss of his sweetened tea, he grabbed up his rifle and peered through the gathering dusk, trying to spot that wanton disturber of his peace.

"Oh, you leetle damn t'ing!" he fumed. "W'ere are you? Jus' come out w'ere I can see you. Pierre won' hurt you. *Non, non.* Come on out and sit op and get your peecture took'n."

The vexatious thing, however, very meanly refused to come out and sit up and pose for its picture. It remained where it was— hidden somewhere in that debris up the hillside.

To locate it more precisely, Pierre blew a quick note and listened closely. Back came a *squink*. It came from that big hump of logs and rocks a hundred yards away.

As cautiously as though he were stalking a brown cannibal bear of the glaciers, Pierre slipped a few steps up the slope, blew again, listened again. *Squink*—as brazen and insolent as ever.

With the whistle between his lips and with rifle at alert, he started for the débris hump, stealthily, asking only for one glimpse of that insulting mocker.

Every few steps he would stop, blow, listen, and hear that answering *squink*.

He reached the edge of the débris, stepped cautiously upon a log, blew one last note on his willow whistle, and waited.

No *squink* came that time. Instead, from that dark tangle and scarcely arm's reach away, came the metallic *snick* of a trigger safety being snapped on "red"; and from behind that *snick* came a human voice, sharp and steely, in knife-edge French:

"*Vous-là! Élevez-vous! Vite! Un, deux, trois*"…

CHAPTER SIXTEEN

FROM the supper fire Flood accompanied Harla to the little cabin which he had fixed up comfortably and given her for the night, till he could get her away from this headwaters camp.

As they walked those thirty yards through the chill twilight, Flood talked to her confidentially about the placer below the cliff.

"I couldn't tell you this in front of those men of mine," he said, "but I intend to skim the cream off that strike down there and then fade. Before snow flies I can lift a million dollars out of that hole. I hate to leave the rest of it, six or seven millions at the least, lying right there for the taking; but it's dangerous to keep an outfit in *défendu* country very long. Some wandering Smoky might see and blab. If those Dinokuis were out of the road so that this territory would be thrown open to legal prospecting—— But there's no hope of that, now."

In spite of her numbing weariness, Harla's attention was caught by that remark about the Dinokuis being out of the road. She wondered . . . Had Flood made a calculated attempt to get this region flung open to exploitation? Had *he* sent the white man and sick *métis* down to that fishing party, in a deliberate move to wipe out the Dinokuis?

She believed he had done just that. Those Dinokuis had stood between him and six or seven million dollars; and at long distance, without actually putting his own hand to the job. he had tried to get rid of them.

"A whole band of innocent people—men and women and children," she thought; and Flood's hands on her arm made her shudder.

"These men of mine," Flood added, "can stick here and get nabbed if they want to, but not I. A cool clean million, and I'm gone. It's Europe for me. That is, I'll begin with Europe."

As he went on and on, speaking with eager enthusiasm about France and Tripoli and the Levant, Harla tried to figure out why he was taking her into his confidence like this. He had some subtle purpose for it, and for his kindly treatment of her since her arrival here a few hours ago.

She could well understand his own thirst for the sunlit life he was sketching. Beneath his bravado Flood was a frightened and hunted man. Weary of his shadowy and fugitive existence, weary of a criminal's hardships, he wanted haven, somewhere, from that perpetual menace of the gallows.

But why was he telling *her* about his hopes and plans?

By the time they reached the cabin door she had caught his drift. He was expecting her to brood about these happy pictures of sunny lands and a soft luxurious life. At the lonely mountain camp where he was taking her tomorrow, she would have plenty of time and mood for such thoughts. He seemed confident that his courteous treatment would gradually change her opinion of him. Without saying so now or risking an explosion from her, he was trying to implant the idea that she could share his million and happy vista—if she wished.

The suggestion was so fantastic that she wanted to answer it by seizing the automatic in Flood's pocket and using the gun on him. But she kept stern hold of herself. The attempt might fail. It was not the deadly sure opening which she had sworn to wait for. If she kept her head and lulled Flood's suspicions, her chance would come with the inevitability of fate—tomorrow, next week, next month.

At the little cabin Flood opened the door and motioned for her to enter.

It took all of Harla's will power to step across that threshold. She knew that this cabin had been Jimmy's. The large cabin yonder, where the men were staying, was newly built, by Flood's party; but this one, more than a year old, had been Jimmy's wilderness home, built by his own hands. This place would be haunted tonight for her.

"I'll fix a good fire for you," Flood said, going in with her. "This up country is cold of evenings."

He lit a candle, stirred the coals in the little sheet-iron stove and put in fresh wood. He wanted to linger and talk; but Harla bade him a peremptory good night.

At the door he turned and said courteously: "Try to sleep, Harla. You're tired out." By way of telling her that escape was impossible, he added, "If you should want more wood or something to eat—you hardly touched your supper—there'll be one of my men just outside." He nodded good night and left.

Alone, fighting against a dread of being alone under that roof, Harla glanced around the cabin: at the little stove, puffing cheerily and growing red along its sides; at the log walls, carefully fitted and chinked; at the small parchment window; at the bunk where Flood had unrolled his own warm eider poke for her.

The whole place brought her poignant memories of a small play-cabin, years ago in Ontario, which she and a little dictatorial boy had built, and where she had played with Indian and *métis* children.

She moved over to the bunk and sat on the edge of it, trying to get courage to snuff the candle and lie down. Fresh in her ears, Flood's earnest talk of a few minutes ago kept flouncing in and out of the turmoil of her mind. His talk had given her a deep look into the man himself, and what she saw there dealt her one of the profoundest shocks of her twenty-six years. Hitherto she had regarded Flood as a thoroughly vicious and inhuman person, but now she perceived that he was all too human and that the motives driving him were widespread in the society from which he sprang.

His thirst for a "cool clean million" was identical with the thirst which she had seen in scores of men. Her own brother Jimmy had been afflicted with it and had lost his life because of it. If that thirst had led Flood to crime, it had also led other men to a blind sacrifice of precious values and to careers essentially predatory even if they were within the law.

And Flood's personal vanity, his desire to be a "big shot" in the eyes of other people, especially of women—he shared that vanity and desire with half the men she knew.

What had his thirsts and motives brought him? Even though he had been successful beyond the dreams of the ordinary criminal, his way of life had burned out with him and he was unspeakably weary of it. His prowling and light-o'-loves had likewise burned out. He wanted a settled life and one woman's love. After a career of crime he was trying to sneak back into the company of decent men.

In a little while she forced herself to lie down on the bunk; but she removed Flood's sleeping-poke, and left the candle burning. The whisper of wind around the eaves, the creaking of the lodgpole rafters, the flickering shadows against the walls, preyed so badly on her tired imagination that she could not bear the dark.

As she lay quiet, thinking, she prayed that Noel really had been arrested and taken to Fort James, as Flood said. If Noel was free, he would come after her. Against Flood's formidable outfit he stood no chance. They would kill him, as they had killed Jimmy. He probably knew this perfectly well but he would come anyway. He was of that sort. After all her repeated snubbings, her cruel suspicions, and then that visit to the way-cabin, he still would gamble with his life to save her.

What hurt her the worst, as she looked back across those stormy weeks with Noel, was the fact that just when he had desperately needed her friendship, she had completely failed him. In his love for her there had been a kind of hunger which tugged at her when she thought about it now. He had never had the friends and golden freedom and rich associations that she had had. For a period half the span of her lifetime, Noel had been a shadow, living and associating with men of the shadows. In the line of duty he had been gangster, dope runner on the Coast, silk smuggler, foreign operative. He had been everything that one could think of, and he had been sent everywhere, from Shanghai to the European capitals. Homeless, uprooted, he had lived a harsh, austere life, with hardly one real friend or human contact.

And then, she had failed him. A splendid chance had been given *her*, of all the people Noel had ever met. She could have been a kind of emotional haven to him, after those shadow years. But she had been blind to that chance and had flung it away. In the Grand Marais and on the *Midnight Sun* he had wanted her, but that time was past now, like the blossom day of a flower. It had ended with that visit of hers to the way-cabin ....

Into her weary thoughts, as she was sinking toward sleep, crept a whisper, low and hollow, coming from nowhere, mingling with the eerie sibilance of the wind.

"Harla!"

The whisper jarred her wide awake. It frightened her so much—fitting into her imaginations—that she dared not look around or even open her eyes.

The whisper came again, cautious but impatient. "Harla!" And then: "For heaven's sake, come alive, girl! D'you hear me?"

She sat bolt upright and stared wildly around the cabin, trying to locate the source of that hollow whisper.

"Keep quiet!" it warned. "Here—I'm here by the window."

Harla looked at the window and saw the glitter of a knife blade. Slowly, noiselessly, the knife was working down along a side of the casement, cutting the parchment out of the single pane.

"Noel—?"

"*Quiet!* There's a man five steps from your door. Snuff that candle and tiptoe over here."

The sound of Noel's voice, the knowledge that he had come for her and was with her again, sent a wild surge of joy through Harla. With trembling hands she lifted the candle and blew it out, and then tiptoed hastily across the dark cabin.

"Are you alone, Noel?"

"Yes." He slit the last few inches of the parchment and lifted it from the window. "You can squeeze through, now. I'll help you. No noise—your guard, around there, is an Indian."

For all her gladness over Noel's coming and all her wish to be with him, Harla hung back. If he tried to get her away, he would likely pay for it with his life; and the mere thought of his getting killed made her panicky.

And she herself scarcely wanted to be free. Escape would mean losing her contact with Flood, and that contact was her one hope of avenging Jimmy.

"Noel, I can't let you do this," she objected, in whispers. "I can't let them kill you, and that's what'll happen. Flood's got nine men here——"

"And I've got a whole platoon! Don't worry about me. Come on."

"A platoon? You just said you were by yourself."

"Don't waste time arguing. Here, give me your hand."

Harla refused. "Noel, please. Please, go away while you still can. I'm safe enough. Flood has treated me decently."

"What's that? Safe? With *him*? Good Lord, what's gone the matter with you, girl? Have you let a bit of initial suavity blind you? If you won't come for your own sake, come for mine. You can do me a supreme favor, if you will."

"What?"

"Let's get clear of this cabin, and I'll tell you about it."

She gave in, but only because it was Noel who was asking it of her.

For a moment, as he helped her through the narrow window, she was in his arms, and that moment brought her flashes of the times in the Grand Marais when he had comforted and buoyed her up. She remembered the touch of his lips upon her hair, and she half expected him to kiss her now, if only because they were together again, partners against Flood's men. But he did not. Even her whisper of gratitude and her squeeze on his arm, as he stood her down, went unanswered.

He reached for a rifle leaning against the logs and handed it to her, with an extra clip of cartridges.

"Here. You likely won't need this, but you'll feel better by having it."

"But you haven't any gun."

"I've my automatic—and that platoon. Let's be traveling."

In cautious silence they started down the winding trail toward the cliff.

"I could hardly believe it when I saw you down there at the supper fire," Noel remarked, to the silent-footed girl beside him. "Why hasn't Flood taken you away, Harla?"

"He's had no chance yet. His canoe party got here with me late this evening."

"You mean last evening."

"No, *this* evening. You see, at the start of that trip they tied me up, but they got tired of carrying me across those long hard totes, and they let me walk, and I watched my chance and made a break. I was halfway back to the Dinokui island before they caught me again, twenty hours later. If it hadn't been for that Indian tracker, they wouldn't ever have caught me."

"Hmmph! You're a queer bundle of contradictions, girl. Yesterday you risked bullets to make a break, and tonight, with a wide-open chance, I had to argue you into it!"

"I changed my mind."

"You'd better start changing it back again. When day comes on, and that'll be within an hour, hell a-plenty will probably break loose here. Flood has been trying for weeks to force a showdown battle on me; and this time I'm holding a half-decent hand. Whatever happens, I'll put a first-class crimp in his style. Herm Spencer won't have much left to do but mop up."

Harla gripped his arm. "Noel! You're not going to fight that outfit? I won't let you! It'd be suicide. Those men are bush-wise as weasels, and they're fine shots, too. In a rifle battle it's bush-experience and marksmanship that count, and you're poor at both."

He said nothing to that. Halfway between the cabin and the cliff he stopped on the trail and pointed up the steep brushy slope.

"The place that I selected for my 'pill-box' is up yonder, a few steps. Let's get off this path and go up there, and then I'll give you complete instructions."

"Instructions?" Harla echoed. A hot rebellion welled up in her as she grasped Noel's plain intentions. He meant not only to stay and fight Flood's outfit but to shunt her completely aside. "Look here, Noel Irving—you're not going to cover any back trail for me! If you think so, then you'd better start changing *your* mind. Before I'd let you do that, I'd go and climb back into that cabin."

Noel merely said, "Hmmph," and led her on up the dark slope.

Thirty yards above the trail he stopped at a little nest of boulders and windfall, partly screened with buckbrush.

"This is my pill-box," he remarked, stepping down between the granite blocks. "It's got more openings in it than I like, more places where lead bumblebees can come whizzing through; but it was the best I could find in a hurry, and it gives me an unobstructed sweep of that camp down there."

As Harla followed him into the granite nook, she saw an odd three-legged contraption squatting in the little space. In the darkness she could distinguish merely a tripod outline and a star-gleam on metal.

"What's that thing, Noel?"

"My platoon."

Puzzled, Harla bent over it and looked closer; timidly reached out and touched it; felt of its big water-jacketed barrel; ran her fingers along a belt of cartridges.

"Noel!" she gasped, bumping her head against his shoulder as she straightened up. "That's a machine gun!"

"Right. Moreover, it's an old friend of ours—the Vickers from that gray plane. I unbolted it and took it out of the ship and lugged it up here. Flood's half-breed guard is lying in that avalanche débris, tied up. Wine, woman and song are said to be fatal to any good job, and his particular weakness was music."

That "woman" sounded to Harla as though Noel was taking a thrust at himself for bringing her into the North and allowing her to get involved in his hunt. It angered her to be cataloged, along with wine and song, as a fatal weakness. It hurt her even worse to see that Noel was looking back on their relationship with such cold and cynical eyes.

He motioned her to sit down on a granite block, but she refused. Confronting him, she demanded, point-blank:

"Noel, what are you planning to do here?"

"I haven't any definite plans. I've been taking things as they come, on this trip; and so far they've come lucky. I do have a scheme in mind to pry Flood away from those men. If it works, it'll save bloodshed. If it doesn't work, why then"—he laid his hand on the cold Vickers—"then I'll do all the damage I can to this pack."

"If you're bound and determined on a fight," she broke out, "I'm going to be in on that." She wanted nothing more than to look down a rifle barrel at Flood, and a fight would give her that chance. "Don't forget that I can handle a gun. We'll either escape together or I'm staying here. You can take your choice."

To her ultimatum Noel paid no attention. He seemed granite-hard. As though she had not spoken at all, he went calmly ahead:

"The favor you can do me is to take a message in to Manitou. A message from me to Spencer. There is something that Herm has got to know. By himself he might never suspect it or believe it; but if you tell him that *I* said so, then he'll believe it and act on it."

Harla started to fling at him again that she was not going, but something in Noel's manner silenced her. His slow grim words made her blood run cold. He was making arrangements against death. "A message from me to Spencer"—he was passing the baton to another man, fully realizing that in a showdown battle, alone against that outfit, he was going to get killed.

He leaned her rifle against a windfall and motioned again at the granite rock. "Please—while I give you this message." He glanced at the camp, still dark and asleep; then at the northeastern sky, streaked with the first faint gray. "You've got to be going," he said. "I'll speak fast. There's considerable to tell."

He crouched down beside her, his hand on her arm. The wan light of the moon rested on his face; and as Harla gazed at him her eyes dimmed with tears and she reached out unthinkingly and smoothed his hair. He seemed so careless of living, so alone and gloomy … It stabbed her to realize that she had contributed so heavily to his gloom. She wanted to plead with him to blot out everything that was past between them, and get out of this valley of death with her, and go away; but she knew he would never go, and she kept silent.

"I'll back up to the beginning of this story," he said, "so that you'll get it straight. It starts thirteen years ago, exactly when I entered the Mounted Police.

"That same summer, Harla, a certain youngster came out of the Manitoba Strong-Woods, where he'd been born and raised, and went to Winnipeg, and got connected with a shady mining concern there. Because of his experiences in the Flin-Flon and other mining districts, he was quite adept at small-time wildcatting. Just when the law was reaching out to nab him, he dropped from sight and was rumored dead. What really happened, he shed his name and identity and past, as cleanly as a snake sheds its skin, and vanished across the Border to Minneapolis.

"After several years of crime there, he got on another hot spot. A bad one. If the law had taken him, Harla, he would have burned. But the law didn't. He got killed. In a gangster quarrel. Then, from Minneapolis, he drifted on down to Chicago——"

Harla blinked her eyes at that. "Why, Noel, you said he got killed!"

"Officially, yes. To be considered dead is the day-dream of every hunted criminal; and he had a genius for working that dodge. But let me go on.

"When he emerged again from obscurity, like a death's-head moth from its cocoon, he was a big-time criminal, a gang leader and the most tantalizing personage that the Federals or Mounted ever dealt with. There was no actual physical evidence that such an individual even existed, Harla. He was never captured, fingerprinted, pictured or adequately described. Some good men on both Forces firmly believed that this person was all a myth—a kind of corporation title behind which several brainy criminals were veiling their identities.

"The explanation of his shadowiness is simple. He seldom appeared on an actual job. His men did it. And whenever the Federals closed in on his outfit, he escaped by double-crossing his men, leaving them holding the bag, while he himself faded. Somehow or other he tapped wires on both the Federals and Mounted, knew their codes and plans, and so could keep several jumps ahead.

"I was called home from Shanghai to take this man. Last March I trapped him, with Spencer's help, in a cabin hangout south of Winnipeg. Spencer and I did an infinitely careful job of trailing and cornering him. He had slipped out of so many squeezes, left so many of his gangs to be killed, that Herm and I went to absurd lengths to make *positive* that this time we had him."

It dawned on Harla, then, that Noel was speaking of Frank Rocco. She had never heard this inside story of the notorious desperado, and the account fascinated her, coming from the lips of the man who had killed him.

Noel paused a moment, as though thinking of that blizzardy March night last spring.

"For certain humane reasons," he replied, "I slipped up to that cabin by myself, with a bundle of short-fused dynamite, and scattered Rocco's hangout all over the lake shore. With that I thought the case was ended. I never doubted, never questioned. It never entered my mind that Rocco might not have been in that cabin when I blew it up."

Harla gasped. "Noel! Are you saying that Rocco might have slipped away again?"

Noel shook his head, slowly, like a person with a torment in his brain. "I don't know. God, I actually don't know. I'm not saying positively that he slipped us, but that's my belief now. Harla, I believe Frank Rocco is still alive."

Harla shook his arm. "Noel, don't allow yourself to think that!" His doubts, his raging uncertainty, made her suspect that he had brooded too long on the disastrous Rocco case. "You yourself killed Rocco. Everyone knows you did. The official investigation proved that you did. He was buried. He's dead."

"Maybe! And maybe he slipped us and shed his skin again. Maybe, with the mid-West too hot for him, and with no money to go abroad, he decided to hit for the oblivion of his native North. Maybe he got wind of a youngster at Manitou with a rich mining prize, and collected another outfit, and——"

Harla sprang to her feet, stunned by his words even though she utterly disbelieved them. "Noel, stop! Stop it! Don't let your imagination run wild like that." With wide eyes she stared at him, at the red campfire in the dark valley, at the black pine drogue hiding the big cabin where Flood was lying asleep. "Flood—Rocco...It *can't* be! Noel, don't say that or think it. You're tired and overwrought and—and——"

"——and crazy?" Noel completed, calmly. "That's what I thought when the idea first struck me. I laughed at it. But I'm not laughing now. If we had time, I could give you several hard-fact items linking Rocco to Flood—items that you can't laugh off. It's my opinion that when you pull the mask from Flood, you'll see nobody but Frank Rocco. He's changed, maybe—older, shrewder, tired of outlawry; but the same man."

Because she knew of the Rocco myth and of the pernicious harm it had done, Harla understood, at last, the forces that were driving Noel to this battle. He wanted to wipe out the mistake he had made and to end that poisonous myth. The granite hardness which she had seen in him was his grim intent that either he or Spencer was going to take Flood back to the city country, prove up his career, strip all his glory clothes off and expose him as a sordid killer. With a cold impersonality, Noel was sinking himself, his own wishes and his very life, in a greater issue. He was looking upon himself and his fine-tempered sword as a weapon in the hands of destiny.

"What I've told you," Noel concluded, "is what I want you to tell Herm Spencer. That's the favor I'm asking of you. If it isn't in the cards for me to do the job, tell Herm that I want him to take Flood alive, thoroughly investigate and uncover the man, and then *hang* him."

He picked up the rifle and offered it to Harla. "And now you must be going. You've time enough but none to spare. There's a canoe at the lower end of the lake. It's fast and light; you can carry it over those totes easily; you can be down at the Dinokui island in twelve hours. These men can't follow. I slit their two canoes, and besides they'll have their hands plenty full here, with me and this machine gun."

Harla cut him short. "I tell you I'm not going! You came up here to save me, and now I'm not sneaking off and leaving you to pay the bill. I'm staying here and helping you."

"I don't need your help. If this Vickers can't bring me through, nothing can."

"That Vickers won't. A machine gun makes a lot of noise and throws a lot of lead around, but it doesn't amount to much in a bush fight. One hit, one bullet placed where you want it, is worth a thousand misses. Those men down there are superb shots, Noel. They'll scatter, they'll start sniping at you, and that'll be your finish."

"Well," he said, "if your diagnosis is correct, I don't see any sense to your staying here and getting rubbed out, too."

"I do! You and I together would have a chance of coming through alive. You by yourself would not. But why does either of us have to stay?" Her hands crept up to his shoulders, and she pleaded: "Noel, let's both go. We can. We can go together. We broke away from those men once, in country worse than this. We can save ourselves and get back to Manitou, and then you can take up your hunt again."

Noel shook his head. "Flood would know I've been here. He'd fade. He'd never come back. I'd lose him. After all, I'm sitting here with a machine gun trained on their camp, and that's a grip I won't let go of. At the least I'll smear that outfit up so bad that they'll be easy meat for Spencer. I've got to stay."

"All right, if that's your decision." She leaned the rifle against the windfall and resolutely sat down. "I'm staying too. You're not going to be my bullet-proof vest just because I'm a girl."

For a long moment Noel looked at her in helpless silence. Then: "There at Manitou, in Alice's cabin, I tried to argue with you, just as I'm doing now. If you'd have listened to me then, if you'd have gone back south, you wouldn't have been captured, I wouldn't be here, we wouldn't be in this fix. But you wouldn't listen, and here we are. You threw a monkey wrench into my hunt——"

"Yes, I did," Harla admitted. "But it's thrown now, Noel; and I'm not going to let you pay for my blindness."

"Then square your mistake by taking my message in to Manitou."

"*No!*"

In the darkness she could not see Noel's face but she could fairly feel the reproach of his gaze. Against her immovable stand there was nothing he could do.

"You're not fooling me any, Harla," he said, "about your chief motive for staying here. You want to drive a bullet at Flood." He picked up the rifle, as though wanting to keep the gun in his own hands. "This fight is bigger than any personal feud. That little vengeance bullet of yours would do a mountain of harm."

After a bitter struggle with herself, Harla looked up at him and promised, "If—if you'll make peace with me, Noel, I'll forego that bullet."

"I don't believe it. You'd forget your promise, you'd break it, you'd doublecross——"

"Noel!"

"I'm sorry. Forgive me."

"Do you take my promise?"

No answer from him.

"Do you, Noel?" she urged. And then: "You may as well take it, Noel, for it's all you're going to get from me. I'm staying."

He was silent in defeat.

"Please give me the rifle, Noel."

"You won't shoot," he asked, reluctantly, helpless against her decision, "even if you see Flood getting away?"

"I promise I will not."

"And even if the fight goes against us?"

"Even if the fight goes against us."

Silently he handed her the rifle.

CHAPTER SEVENTEEN

WHILE the slow dawn came on, they plugged up the worst openings in their pill-box and arranged the loose windfall into a sort of breastworks.

The gray light broadened till they made out the log buildings in the drogue below and saw Flood's sentry, a Yellowknife Indian, sitting on a boulder in front of Jimmy's cabin.

The wilderness gradually stirred and yawned and woke. On a solitary snag up slope a golden eagle flexed its stiffened wings and launched itself on the day's hunt. Up valley a band of goats, driven to the high rocks by the night-roaming wolves, tripped daintily back down toward timberline and fell to browsing in a patch of moraine green. The bright morning sun was striking full against the western fields of ice and snow; and under its melting warmth the glacier torrents, nearly stilled during the chill of night, started murmuring again, louder and louder, swelling toward their midday mountain song.

After carefully inspecting the Vickers and planting rocks against the tripod, Noel crept over beside Harla. With her rifle thrust through a chink, she was lying flat behind a boulder, watching the camp below.

"Cold?" he asked.

"My hands are, a little bit. I wish I had pockets, like you. These granite rocks are like ice."

"I'll fix you up. We need our trigger fingers in good shape." He took her right hand, cupped it in his and blew on it. "That help any?"

"A lot—thanks."

He felt her hand trembling and saw that she was badly frightened. For all her wild-Indian girlhood and tomboyish experiences, she was a gentle girl at heart; and this life-and-death battle looming up had awed and shaken her.

He hoped she would not go to pieces when the fight broke open. If she shot with her usual deadliness, she would be of tremendous help. Strange that she, who had never heard the *zz-ing* of a bullet meant to kill or felt the hot shock of a bullet striking her, should be a dead-shot, while he himself, who could have filed half a dozen notches on his black automatic, was only ordinary with a gun.

At last two men emerged from the big cabin in the drogue. One was young Paul d'Orleans. The other was a thin smallish white man of forty-five, who had been one of the contestants at the McMurray rifle match.

"Who is that older man, Harla?"

"The others call him Jed. He's Flood's lieutenant. He and Paul are our two bad ones, Noel. They're both extraordinary shots. If your plan doesn't work and we have to fight, we ought to get them first. But I wish that young Paul was out of this."

That same wish rested with Noel. Young and thoughtless, Paul d'Orleans had hooked up with Flood in a spirit of adventure, exactly as so many city youngsters of good mettle were victimized by the false glamour of a lawless life.

After throwing fresh wood on the campfire coals, young d'Orleans strode over to the torrent, peeled off his leather shirt and lustily splashed water over himself, snorting like a young bull moose; but the man called Jed crouched down at the fire and spread his hands to the warmth of the flames.

Young d'Orleans came back and started to cook breakfast. As he worked he kept talking, joking; and some remark from him made his companion laugh. At that laugh Noel stiffened and his face went hard. He had heard that evil laugh before—out of the mist and moonlight of a Winnipeg night. It resurrected a memory, vivid as a lightning flash, of Jimmy clutching at his breast and sinking to the floor. Wantonly this man had laughed then, in confidence that he and his shadowy confederates could never be trailed and made to pay.

"Harla"—he touched her arm—"for certain reasons I want *you* to get that man there. We may never walk out of this valley alive, but neither must he!"

After ladling the food into tin plates, young d'Orleans picked up a stick of wood and sent it whanging against the door of the big cabin.

"You, in dere!" he yelled. "Pile out of dem pokes, you lazy sons of a blue bull-mink. How you speck to tom-rock yourself a t'ousan' dollar wort' of dust today if you poun' de ear till noon? Make it sneep-snap, or I'll eat op all your breakfusses myself!"

The rest of the men came outside, sleepy-eyed, pulling on their shirts and jackets as they came; and Noel had his first look at Flood's formidable outfit.

Ranging all the way from city whites to that dusky Yellowknife, they were a queer assortment of men to be running in the same pack. Only Flood's genius at gang leadership could have welded them into a tight smooth-working group. Each in his own fashion, they were outstanding individuals, picked for some special quality. Besides the man called Jed, and young d'Orleans, who was hunter and guide, and the Yellowknife, who was tracker and bush-scout for the party, there were two Nahanni half-breeds and three whites and Flood himself.

Of those white men one was a shaggy-haired northern pros-pector, exuberant of spirit, like Paul d'Orleans. He evidently was boss of the placer workings; and those two huge Nahannis, as big and lumbersome as bears, were his chief helpers.

The other two whites looked to Noel like products of a city alley. One was the pilot whom he had seen at Manitou. The other was Flood's machine gunner.

After nodding good morning to his men and telling them to "hit that placer hard today," Flood beckoned the pilot aside and talked with him alone, evidently making arrangements to fly Harla away from there.

Noel looked at Harla and saw her fingers tighten on the rifle barrel as she gazed down at Flood; and he was afraid that in the passion of a hot battle she would forget her solemn promise and drive a bullet at the man, especially if he tried to sneak out of the fight and get away.

After his talk with the pilot, Flood started for Jimmy's place; and as he neared it he said to the Yellowknife sentry, who was still guarding the empty cabin:

"Thanks for watching here, Stahmix. Go and get your breakfast. I want you to slip down the Dinokui River today and keep an eye on that *Shagalasha* detail, and find out, if you can, whether this Lanier man is under arrest."

He strode on to the cabin and knocked.

Noel motioned down at the camp. "Lord, what a layout, Harla—what a perfect layout for us, if we wanted to take it!" There they were, all those men, close around that breakfast fire and wide open to the Vickers. He could get them all, the whole pack, with one long burst; and Flood, thirty yards from them, was entirely out of the danger zone. In his hands lay a chance such as he had never remotely dreamed of when he broke arrest and started up the Dinokui alone. Within the space of twenty seconds he could destroy that entire outfit and take Flood alive and avoid all danger of a battle, in which Harla might get killed.

Debating fiercely, he glanced at the camp, then at Harla, beside him. Her life was infinitely more precious than the lives of those eight. Murder, poison and machine guns, and then their unspeakably brutal attempt to wipe out a tribe of harmless innocent people—they had forfeited all right to mercy.

He turned toward the Vickers, to seize his fine chance before it passed. But Harla stopped him.

"Noel, don't! Don't make a shambles of that breakfast fire. It'd be too much like murder. Give them a chance to take your terms, Noel. If they turn you down and start the fight themselves, then we won't have any blood-guilt on our hands."

At the little cabin Flood knocked twice; and when he got no answer he opened the door an inch and peered inside. With a startled oath he flung the door wide and stepped upon the threshold.

For moments he stood there, stock-still, a picture of dumb-founded surprise, staring at the sleeping-poke on the floor, at the bunk, the slashed-out window.

With no great effort Noel could imagine the man's thoughts. That empty cabin was a double-barreled disaster to Flood. He had lost not only Harla but the placer too, for if Harla escaped down river to the Mounted detail and told them about him, he would have to abandon his rich prize and clear out of the North altogether.

Flood whirled around, presently, and looked at the camp-fire, at the Indian to whom he had entrusted the guarding of that cabin; and his fists clenched and unclenched as he glared at the Yellowknife.

Harla slipped her trigger safety on red. "We'd better be get-ting ready for trouble. He'll put that Indian to tracking us."

"If he puts that Indian anywhere, it'll be on the fire to broil," Noel answered, as Flood left the cabin and hurried back the path. He did not fully realize how murderous a rage had seized Flood, but he did know fury when he saw it.

"If you're going to run a burst and drive them into that cabin," Harla bade, "you'd better be doing it."

"Steady a minute. Watch down there. We might get a break out of this."

As Flood neared the campfire the men looked up at him, stopped eating and glanced sidelong at one another, aware that something catastrophic had happened. The unsuspecting

Yellowknife had just set his rifle against a tree, and his back was turned; and upon him, without word or warning, Flood sprang like a furied tiger. With a grab he tore the Indian's knife and belt ax away, flung them into the fire, and staggered the Indian with a smashing blow to the face. Grappling the Yellowknife by the throat, he rode the Indian to the ground and pinioned him there, with his knee on the Indian's chest and his fingers tightening their strangle-hold.

All the other men, all save young d'Orleans, were paralyzed by the violence of Flood's outburst, and they could only stare at the two. But d'Orleans, dropping his plate and fork, leaped up and rushed in.

"Hey! W'at de hell?" he cried, grabbing Flood by the shoulders. "Flood! Stop dat! You gone crazy, *hein?* Get off dis feller. Leave go, you!"

Flood loosened one hand and struck at young d'Orleans, but the latter tore him away from the Indian and locked his arms behind him.

"Flood! Don'! Easy, Flood," he argued, as Flood struggled to break out of his powerful grip. "Quiet down. You don' keel dis feller wit'out anyhow saying w'y so."

While Flood fought to tear free, the Yellowknife scrambled to his feet and leaped for his rifle. Before anyone could stop him or even move, he had seized the weapon and whipped it up and aimed it at Flood. He too had a fury within him, the blood-fury of an Indian disgraced. And there was no one to halt him from killing Flood. He was yards from those other men, yards from young d'Orleans.

Helpless, stunned, Noel stared down at the spectacle in cold fright. In that tense drama yonder he saw a tragic end to all his hopes of taking Raphael Flood alive. The scene, as it hung poised for an instant, was burned into his brain: the Indian with that rifle butt against his cheek; Flood fumbling for his pocket gun;

young d'Orleans futilely holding up a hand in a wordless entreaty for the Yellowknife not to shoot.

Cr-aa-ck—beside Noel, a sharp-speaking rifle. Harla's. She had been holding her gun at alert, watching over the sights; and she beat the Yellowknife to the trigger squeeze. Carelessly, hardly appearing to take aim at all, she shot once.

Her once was enough. Her bullet caught the Yellowknife hard in the left shoulder, spun him around and knocked him against a sapling. The gun flew from his hands. He staggered and sank to his knees.

In profound gratitude Noel turned to Harla and laid his hand on her arm. He wanted to thank her for pulling his hunt back from sure doom, but he could find no words to say it. He wanted to ask forgiveness for believing that she might break her promise to him. With a splendid loyalty to the spirit of that promise, she had gone far beyond the letter of her pledge. When everyone else was powerless, she had actually saved Flood from death.

As he looked at her, he saw tears spring to her eyes at sight of the reeling and pain-convulsed Yellowknife.

"Stop it!" he ordered her, dismayed at her giving way like that. "You only winked him. He can be patched up. Sympathy for anybody in that outfit is sympathy wasted. It's few tears they'll shed for you and me if they put us out. They'll *laugh*."

The startling bark of Harla's rifle, from the silence of the hillside, yanked the attention of the men from the quarrel between Flood and Stahmix. All of them jumped up and stared blankly at the timbered slope, bewildered by that mystery shot.

Again young d'Orleans was the first to act.

"You, dere!" he shouted. "Who de hell? Speak op, feller!"

Noel tilted the Vickers downward. Harla's shot had touched off the fuse to this struggle, and that fuse could not be pinched now. His cue was to drive all the terror he could into those men while they were so befuddled. Panicky and confused, they might take his terms.

Bracing himself to steady the big gun, he aimed carefully—into the trees above the men; and pulled back on the sheathed trigger.

The sudden burst of staccato fire leaping from the hillside; the storm of bullets *splaating* through the pines; the bellowing roar that filled the narrow valley like long rolling thunder—it created all the pandemonium he had counted on, and more. The shag-haired prospector stumbled backwards and fell over, as though knocked down by a tangible blow. Young d'Orleans sprang for shelter of a boulder. In terror of those screaming bullets Flood whirled and scurried for the cabin and dived into it like a panicky rabbit; and after him streamed the other men, yelling, piling up at the doorway, fighting and pushing to get inside.

Noel cut his burst short, before the last man was within the cabin. He had only two belts; and if his plan failed he would need every inch of them.

In half a minute, as the last faint echoes of the blast died away, he called down:

"Paul d'Orleans! D'you hear me?"

"*Ou', Ou',*" the young *métis* answered, keeping behind his rock. "W'at you wan'?"

"I want to talk to you. Come up here."

Young d'Orleans snorted scornfully. "You t'ink I'm damn-fool babee, *hein?* I don' stan' op and let you pot me."

"I could have potted you, and all the rest of you, if I had wanted to. The point is, I don't want to. Are you yellow, d'Orleans? Afraid to palaver a person, d'Orleans?"

At the taunt the young *métis* bobbed up like a jack-in-the-box. "Me, yaller?" He vaulted up on the rock, in bold challenging view. "You eat dat 'yaller,' you."

"All right, I'll eat it. But come on up here. You can come and go and you won't be touched. That's a promise."

Young d'Orleans turned toward the cabin. "Hey, Flood, w'at you say? You wan' me go op dere?"

Noel did not catch Flood's answer, but it was evidently yes, for d'Orleans jumped off the rock and walked down the foot-trail and turned up slope toward the pill-box. As he came within a dozen steps Noel ordered him:

"That's close enough. Stay where you are."

"Well, I'm here. W'at you wan'?" d'Orleans demanded, eyeing the covert.

"I want Flood," Noel told him. "I don't want you or those others, but I do want Flood; and I'll get him if I have to kill you and that whole outfit."

"I don' quite unnerstan'."

"I mean simply this: if you and those other men will turn Flood over to me, you can all get out of this country scot-free, and I'll never molest you. That's more decency than you rate, you killers; but I'll give it to you."

Young d'Orleans scowled. "You t'ink we knife Flood in de back lak dat? And give op dat seex-seven million dollar placer down dere jus' 'cause you say so? *Splaa!* We'll give you wan bellyful of fight 'fore we do dat."

"You can't fight. You're sewed up. We've got you trapped in that cabin, you can't get out, we're covering that door and window with a machine gun. Besides that, your two planes down there are out of commission. As for that mine, you haven't a chance in a million to keep it. I told the Mounted about it and they're coming in here——"

"*Splaa!* You didn' tell de Mounted nut'ing 'bout dat placer. You jus' wan' dose seex-seven million dollar for yourself. You talk beeg 'cause you're 'fraid of a fight. You got nobody wit' you but dat Harla girl. I see your tracks w'ere you and her come op dis slope."

"We won't argue. Go back down and tell those others what I've told you. Talk it over and make up your minds. I'll give you fifteen minutes to hand Flood over. If you don't, I'll make kindling wood out of that cabin and kill every man of you."

"Okay, I tell 'em."

With a defiant wave he turned and dropped back to the trail and hurried to the cabin.

"He certainly didn't sound very propitious," Harla commented.

"That's true. But those other men haven't his loyalty. They may surrender Flood to save themselves."

"But the placer, Noel; this 'seex-seven million'—that's where they'll balk."

He nodded. She was dead-right. If his plan smashed, it would smash upon that placer. The gold lust had seized those men and was running hot in their blood. That ancient caldron pool, with its glittering sands and the sizable fortune that it held for every one of them, was something for which they would risk death. Blinded by its golden dazzle, they might refuse to believe that it was forever lost to them, whether they won the fight or not.

Through the slow-dragging minutes he and Harla waited, waited, wondering what was going on in that cabin yonder.

The wounded Yellowknife pulled himself together, went over to the streamlet and bathed his shoulder in the icy water. Except for that they saw nothing of their enemies.

The fifteen minutes passed. Impatient, nervous, Noel trained the Vickers on the cabin window.

"I'd better convince 'em that I mean business," he said. "If they're wavering, a splash of lead might help 'em make up their minds."

He ran a short ten-second burst that splintered the window casing, tore the parchment to shreds, and sent a hail of bullets inside the log building.

He released, listened, watched. At the cabin itself, not a stir, not a sound. But as the echoes of his tattoo dwindled to silence, a yell came flouncing across the valley from a buckbrush ravine beyond and above the cabin. A taunting yell from the lips of young d'Orleans:

"Dat's fine! Do dat ag'in! Dat gun, she make fine-dandy music, but she ain' singing to us!"

Harla turned, pale of face. "Noel! They got out of that cabin! They must've knocked a log out of the back side and faded into the timber!"

He nodded. "That's what they've done. I should have known they'd turn me down. We had our chance to put them out, but we passed it up, and now they're laughing at us—as they laughed at Jimmy."

For a full half hour they heard nothing whatever from their enemies. Over the valley and the steep slopes hung a silence that was ominous of a gathering storm.

The fearful uncertainty of what to expect got on their nerves. In low tones, as they watched and waited, they argued about what those men were doing.

"They're over on that west slope," Harla insisted. "They're hunting places where they can see us and snipe us."

"They're on this east slope," Noel countered. "They're going to rush us."

"Rush a machine gun? They're not that crazy."

"They wouldn't have far to rush. Look here"—he gestured at a rocky ravine on that east slope. Coiling down the hillside from some thick timber above, it was deep and twisty, offering perfect cover, perfect approach; and at its nearest swing it passed within thirty feet of their little refuge. "That's too good a set-up for them to have overlooked. They swung up through that timber and got into that couloir, and they're working down toward us. They can boil out of there and be on top of us in three or four jumps."

The long silence was at last broken, abruptly, by the snarl of a rifle across the valley. A bullet came singing into the covert, whined past Noel's throat, nicked the barrel of the Vickers and buried itself in a windfall log.

"Noel, keep *down!*" Harla pleaded. "You're exposing your-self, to watch that ravine. I told you they're over yonder." With her rifle against her cheek she was peering intently at a small gray cliff straight across the valley from them. "I know just about where that man is, Noel. I saw the sun-glint on his gun when he worked the bolt. He's in that clump of dwarf spruces over there. If he moves again, I can get in a shot."

Noel reached into his pocket for the extra rifle clip and laid it on his hat brim, for Harla's .303. That rifle snarl across the valley proved that she was in for a sniping duel with one enemy at least and likely with two—young d'Orleans and the man called Jed, the two crack shots in Flood's outfit.

But he still believed that the chief attack would be a sudden overwhelming rush from the rock ravine just yonder. Their strat-egy was plain enough now. That sniping from the western slope was only a brainy play to draw his and Harla's attention while death stalked them from the other direction. The main party of those enemies had circled around and slipped into the couloir, up among those dense banksians; and now they were working their way down that wash, closer and closer.

"Noel," Harla bade, "move the Vickers a little; I want to lure a shot from that man over there. I believe he was shooting at the Vickers that first time, trying to put it out of commission."

"But I won't move this gun and have them cripple it, girl. I'd rather move myself! This gun is our one chance of stopping that rush."

"He can't get in a square hit, from his angle. That granite block shields all of the Vickers but the front end of the barrel. Move it just a little bit—please."

Reluctantly Noel swerved the big gun a few inches. Almost instantly that sharp-speaking rifle cracked again. The bullet struck the Vickers' barrel near the bead, jarred the gun but did no harm, caromed off a granite slab and ricocheted up the slope.

The deadliness of that rifle jolted Noel. He glanced at Harla to see whether she had spotted the man. He saw her eyes narrowing and her trigger finger slowly tightening as she firmed her aim. He turned again, quickly, and glanced across at the gray cliff.

Harla shot. At the bark of her gun something threshed violently in those dwarf spruces; a rifle cartwheeled out of the thicket, struck against the cliff-side and clattered on the granites below; a man-figure rolled out of that hiding and tumbled over the rock into the top of a banksian, and bumped from limb to limb to the ground.

The sight of that toppling figure had a bad whipback on Harla. She turned to Noel, white-faced, appalled at what she had done.

"Noel," she sobbed, "that—was—was young Paul." Her rifle dropped from her hands; she seemed on the verge of going completely to pieces.

Noel was frightened. He himself was hopelessly outmatched at this bush-sniping. If he and Harla had any chance at all of fighting off death, that chance rested squarely on her deadly shooting.

"Are you forgetting Jimmy?" he demanded. "Well, I'm not! They murdered him in cold blood and laughed, and now when you shoot one of them in self-defense, you wilt and cry. If you had seen Jimmy standing there by my desk, helpless, gasping when their bullets struck him——"

"Noel! Don't!"

"Snap out of it, then. That rush is going to boil out of the ravine any minute, any second." As Harla picked up her rifle, he added: "This fellow Jed is over there on that hillside somewhere. He's trying to put out our machine gun. Don't let him. You might like to know that he's the man who laughed, there in Winnipeg. What're you going to do if you get a chance at *him?*"

Harla thrust a fresh cartridge into the chamber of her rifle. "I'll—I'll do plenty."

"That's better. I'll try to draw a shot so that you can spot him.

He reached for his hat, put it on the end of a twig and raised it till the crown stuck above the top of the granite boulder.

No shot came. The man Jed, a wary and experienced bush-loper, refused to fall for the ruse.

A few moments later Harla warned, in quick excited tones:

"Noel, that rush *is* coming! You were right! Get ready for it!"

"How d'you know?"

"Take a look at that Yellowknife down there by the water."

Noel flashed a quick glance at the Indian. The man had staunched the bleeding from his wound and slumped down on a log, and was impassively awaiting the outcome of the battle. Toward that outcome he seemed as utterly neutral as the log he was sitting on. One party to that battle had disgraced and tried to kill him; the other party had shot him; and he cared nothing whether this side or that side or both of them got wiped out.

"What do you see odd about him, Harla?"

"Look where he's staring! First at us, then at that gully. He wouldn't stare like that at an empty draw. Those men are in there!"

As though in proof of her words, over at the ravine edge Noel detected a slight stir in the dense brush, at a point a few yards up slope from the twist where he had been expecting the rush to boil out. A moment later a man's head appeared above a talus boulder.

The man was one of those huge Nahanni 'breeds.

After a long look at the little refuge, the 'breed inched down behind the boulder again.

With infinite caution Noel started to swerve the Vickers and train it on the ravine twist where those men were crouching for the rush. Remembering how small a move had drawn a shot from young d'Orleans, he swung the gun with imperceptible slowness, a quarter-inch at a time.

Despite all his precaution, the move drew lightning from across the valley. Whether the sun glinted betrayingly on the big barrel or whether the keen-eyed Jed had already lined aim and would have shot anyhow, he did not know; but from that western slope, from a high jutting knoll to the right of the gray cliff, a rifle spoke out twice, *cr-aa-ck-kk*—two sharp quick shots, so close together that they seemed rolled into one.

Like a hot stab of pain a bullet hit Noel's left forearm, tearing loose his grip on the Vickers, paralyzing his wrist and hand. The second bullet crashed squarely into the feed slot of the gun, smashed the slot and the pawl, and toppled the Vickers over against a rock. On the heels of those two calamitous shots a laugh floated across the valley—a laugh and a triumphant shout from the man Jed:

"You men there—pile in on those two and get 'em! I winged that fellow; I busted that Vickers all to——"

His last word was cut off by the bark of Harla's .303. The mocking shout changed abruptly to an inarticulate yell; and Noel, without turning or looking, knew that Harla had nailed the man Jed as cleanly as she had killed the d'Orleans *métis*.

He flipped the blood from his hand, kicked the useless Vickers out of the way and grabbed out his black automatic.

"Harla! Swing around! The ravine!" he bade. In spite of the turmoil of those moments, he was astounded by the deadliness of Harla's shooting; and it snapped him out of the shock of losing the Vickers. With two lone shots his girl partner had put out two of their enemies, the worst two of all; and that uncanny rifle of hers might stop this rush. He alone could never do it. "Harla! Here! Why don't you swing this way?"

"But Flood—Flood's escaping!" Harla cried. "He ran out of the cabin, he's running down that old river bed, he's heading for the fissure——"

"Let him go! He *can't* get away! I told you that! Here—this full clip—stick it into your rifle!"

As Harla whirled around and thrust in the fresh magazine that he handed her, the rush broke out of the ravine and came crashing down through the deerbush upon them—the pilot and machine gunner, blazing away with automatics at the covert; the prospector swinging a clubbed rifle and yelling in hoarse voice; the two huge Nahannis, belt axes in hand, plowing through the brush like charging grizzlies.

Unable to shoot effectively through the barricade of logs and rocks, Noel and Harla sprang to their feet to meet the rush. In that tumult of yells and oaths and gun fire and the crash of deerbush, Noel heard a cry from Harla, and knew she had been hit; but in the next instant her rifle answered back, a sharp double *cr-aa-ck-kk*; and the machine gunner and one of the Nahannis crumpled, fell—killed instantly at that point-blank range. He himself got a clean chance at the prospector as the latter sprang over a rock, and he took the man out with a blast from the automatic. Five steps from the refuge the pilot stopped short, dropped his empty gun and whirled to flee; but Noel was still hearing that cry from Harla, and he killed the man in his tracks.

The big Nahanni, reaching the very edge of the covert, sprang upon the windfall and arched his belt ax for a murderous blow; but both Noel and Harla had swung their guns on him as he leaped upon the logs; and he toppled dead—inside the refuge itself....

Across his body they looked at each other, in a kind of daze, hardly able to realize that they had stood up to Flood's whole formidable pack and shot it out with them and come out alive. Harla slumped against the barricade, faint and reeling. Noel sprang for her and caught her and kept her from falling.

"Harla! You're hurt!" She was clasping her arm, and the blood was trickling to her fingertips. "Where'd they get you?"

"It—it isn't much," Harla tried to deny, though the pain of her wound was making her gasp. "It—went through—clean. But it—it hurts, Noel—oh, it hurts so bad——"

To get her away from that stricken place, Noel gathered her up, clumsily—his own left arm and hand were numb and awkward; and started down the slope, carrying her.

As he struck the foot-trail and headed for Jimmy's cabin, Harla made him put her down. "Noel, get Flood! I'll make out—by myself—till you get him."

"Good! Go on to that cabin. I'll be gone but a few minutes. When I get back we'll patch ourselves up and whip across to the Big River. In that yellow Albatross. You and I—and Flood—are going in to Manitou!"

He whirled and started back down the path to the fissure.

Through the gallop of his thoughts, as he hurried along, flitted pictures, vivid and prophetic. Of his trip out to the city country with Flood. Of the consternation which this news would cause. Of his entry into Winnipeg with his notorious prisoner. Of the trial that would strip the glory from this man and gibbet him to the public's scorn.

The fiery events of the past few hours had burned away his last doubts about the identity of Raphael Flood. The snake had shed its skin since that bleak March night half a year ago; but it was still the same snake, with the same sinister markings, the same telltale designs. All that Harla had told him about Flood's plans; all that he himself had seen that morning of the man's killer-rage, his cowardice, his betrayal of his men—it all was merely a repetition of what the Federals and he and Herm Spencer had long known about Frank Rocco.

He went down through the fissure, past Jimmy's placer, down the lake shore, and out upon the little willow headland. By the water edge he stood looking at the Albatross, at the shaky and panicky man who was frantically whirring the inertia crank of the plane.

After a few moments he remarked: "That motor might start, Flood, if it had a timer dog in it. But it hasn't. Nor has that gray plane. I took those dogs out last evening when I got your half-breed guard. I knew you'd try to fade. You always have. But this is the time when you don't fade. Just as all the others of your tribe come to sit soon or late, you've come to the end of your trial, *Rocco*."

At that name the man cried out and whirled toward Noel and grabbed blindly for the automatic in his pocket.

"Better drop your gun into the water," Noel advised. "I might have to shoot it out of your hand. And you're shaking so badly that you couldn't hit anything with it anyhow. Don't be so afraid, man. I wouldn't harm you for all the gold in that placer there. *I killed you once, but this time I'm taking you back alive.*"

CHAPTER EIGHTEEN

IN HIS Winnipeg apartment—the same apartment where Jimmy had come to him three months ago—Noel was glancing through a batch of evening papers and reading the press accounts of Flood's conviction that day.

Outside, a reddish October moon, encircled by the hunter's "eye of the buck," shone down upon the boulevard and the shrubbery plot from which those shadows had killed Jimmy and laughed and faded. In the night silence he could hear the trumpeting and gabbling of waterfowl migrating down across the latitudes from that wild Northland where he had spent the most hectic month of his life.

Those men had laughed a bit too soon, he mused, lifting his eyes to the bullet holes still in wall and ceiling. Confident and brazen they had been that night, but now they were dead, all of them but one—their notorious leader. And before the month was out, Flood too would die. No "gallant death" but a common hanging, with all the glamour torn away from him by the pitiless trial just ended.

"Poor devil," Noel muttered, thinking of his last visit to the jail that afternoon and of the broken cringing man who had alternately whined for mercy and cursed him. "He gave it to others a-plenty, but he can't take it himself."

Of the dozen press stories that he glanced at, not one had a word of pity or glorification or excuse for the convicted desperado. "Coward," "slinking killer," "mad dog"—those were a few of the phrases hurled at the master criminal who only last spring had been so glamorous a figure to the man in the street.

For this change of heart Noel was profoundly glad. To a degree that he had scarcely hoped for, the Rocco myth and all its subtle powers for evil were at last exploded, with a bang that was echoing across the Dominion.

Thinking deeply, he laid the papers aside and moved across to the window and stood looking out, grateful that the long trial was over with. He felt little personal triumph in bringing Flood to the gallows, and little elation in the public praise which had beaten upon himself for weeks. He was merely thankful that destiny had put into his hands a heavy weapon for good and that he had brought a sordid career to an end.

As he listened to the migrants in the night sky and watched a high-flying V of cranes wing across the face of the moon, he realized that down in the sub-Arctic the first fall of snow was lying white on tundra and mountain, and the waters were catching over from their long winter sleep. Harla would be getting out of the North before many days. It had been only seven weeks since she had said good-bye to him at Manitou and returned to the Dinokui village, to watch after that strange old people of hers. She had had scant time to make her cherished studies of them, but the Big Dark was coming on and she would have to leave.

He tried to imagine Harla's astonishment when she did return to Ottawa and found him there, heading a Bureau of his own. She would be immensely glad, all right, of his new position—she was true enough a friend for that. But would she be more than a friend to him, there in Ottawa? Which way had the wind been blowing with her since that goodbye at Manitou? To that raging question her two short friendly letters had given no hint at all.

With clear vision he had come to realize, in the past seven weeks, that it was one thing to give Harla DeLong up, as he had done at Manitou, and an abysmally different thing to stop loving her and wanting her. What course was he to take toward her? He could no longer keep that question frozen. Within a few days he was going to Ottawa, where she lived, and he would be there indefinitely, in the same city and social circles, always knowing that she was near him and that the touch of a phone would bring her voice to him.

Whether he stood any chance with her—there was the whole storm-center of his uncertainty. He had little presumption or confidence. That bitter fortnight on the Three Rivers had knocked out all presumption. At times he believed that her emotional attitude toward him had been irretrievably ruined. At other times, looking back on that fortnight from the perspective of many weeks and three thousand miles, he felt that maybe he had been blind to expect friendship from Harla then. Her anxiety about Jimmy and her heartbreak over his death had plunged her into chaos. Under circumstances like those she had had little thought or heart for any friendship.

One thing was certain—in the long weeks since Manitou her feelings toward him had taken definite shape, one way or other. When he saw her again and talked to her, he would *know* ... .

Over at his desk the phone rang. He stepped across and lifted the receiver.

"Noel?"—it was Herm Spencer talking. "Say, Noel, there's a wild and woolly son of the Strong-Woods here with Eleanor and me. He says he's a friend of yours. Says he wants to see you and chew the rag. Maybe you'd better step over for a little while. It's late, I know, but you never go to bed anyway."

"Why, uh, who is he, Herm?" Noel asked. Spencer's jesting tones made him think for a moment that Harla might be there. The midnight Transcontinental from Edmonton had just come in.

"I'll let you talk to him," Herm said. "But come on over, then; we're waiting on you."

In a moment another man's voice came over the wire—a breezy voice which Noel had not heard since leaving the North but which he would have recognized in a stadium crowd.

"Hullo, old-timer! How're you, anyhow?"

"Good heavens—*Strap!* What in the world are you doing in Winnipeg?"

"Haven't done anything yet. Just blew in. But I aim to do plenty before I blow out. Taking a vacation from the old Bellank, and soaking up some sociability."

"So you come to a city to spend your vacation! But I'm not surprised. Not from you."

"What's dizzy about that? It's tit-for-tat—you city bozos come out and burn up our woods for your vacations, so I'm going to burn up your old town for mine! How about dropping around here?"

"Why, yes, Strap. But what about Harla—didn't you bring her out of the North?"

"Sure I brought her, and I didn't crack her up in any mus'rat swamp either, like some people."

"But where'd you leave her? Where is she?"

"I haven't left her anywhere yet. We blew in together and came out here to the Spencers. Want to say hullo to her?"

Noel gasped. All evening he had been thinking of Harla as down in the sub-Arctic; and now, suddenly, here in Winnipeg, with Herm and Eleanor.

Before he could answer Strap's question, he heard Harla take the phone. Afraid to presume on any friendship, he tried to be formal.

"How d'you do, Harla. I hope you had a pleasant trip out——"

That was as far as he got. "Noel!"—a little cry of joy from Harla. It punctured his formality like one of her deadly bullets. The warmth and eagerness of it unsteadied him. "It's so good to hear your voice again, Noel! Strap and I wanted to call you but we couldn't find your number, so we called the

Spencers and they asked us out. Are you busy, Noel? Can you come now?"

"Yes—now," he managed.

As he waited for his taxi, outside, in the moon shadows of a maple, he tried to tell himself that just because a girl was glad to see him he was letting his imagination run wild. Of course Harla was glad, just as she would be glad to see anyone with whom she had shared that week in the Grand Marais and that battle in the ancient river valley.

But he was not sure of this; he could not think straight; his thoughts were all in a whirl at Harla's unexpected coming. As the taxi drew up and he entered it, he felt as though he were launching himself into a white-water stretch, as when he had tilted the Vickers on that enemy camp. It seemed impossible, like a person's life turning on the hapchance flip of a coin, that this next half hour would answer his momentous question, with the bang of finality, and that he could be so utterly in the dark as to what that answer was going to be.

Through the moonlight and smoky haze of the October night; down the interminable boulevard, miles long, hours long; past the cluster of capital buildings; through the flash and blur of innumerable lights; into the quiet of a residential section; and at last the scrunch of brakes, and the driver saying: "Here you are, sir. You don't want your change? Thank you, sir."

As Noel went down the walk, he glanced through the window of the white-tiled kitchen and saw Spencer and Eleanor talking with Strap—chatting and laughing with the Arctic pilot as though they had known Strap for years. He saw nothing of Harla then; but when he stepped into the lighted vestibule he heard quick footsteps, the door opened, he found himself confronting her.

The sight of her was something of a jolt to him. During his weeks with her in the North and in all his thought pictures of her since then, she had been clad in that corduroy woods-suit and laced boots, a rifle in the crook of her arm, her clothes often muddied and bedraggled, especially in the watery wilderness of the Grand Marais. Now she seemed altogether another girl, almost like a stranger whom he had never seen; and that strangeness was what jolted him.

In a velvet frock with gold girdle and buckle, her rebellious black hair smoothed back, gilt slippers, a pendant at her throat, she was so utterly different from his capable partner of the Three Rivers that he scarcely believed she was the same person.

"Noel! Come in!" She took both his hands and drew him in and closed the door with a kick of a slipper. *That* tomboyish act was natural, and it helped him a little against her strangeness. "Why, Noel, don't you know me? What makes you look at me so oddly?"

"Because I never knew"—the words came and he did not halt or try to halt them—"I never knew you were so lovely."

She was not remotely expecting any such remark from him, and it threw her badly into confusion.

The silence was so awkward that Noel tried to retrieve his blunder.

"Pardon me. I didn't mean——"

"No, no—don't you take *that* back!" Harla stopped him. "I won't let you. It's mine; you gave it to me; and you can't have it again!" She had recovered her poise; and her laugh sent the awkwardness skittering. "You wouldn't have said that if you'd seen me twenty minutes ago. I was all but disreputable. I didn't even have a change of clothes. These are Eleanor's."

Noel wondered why she had gone to the trouble of that frock and slippers and all. For his visit? Had she deliberately planned to seem strange and different to him? Different—to the full extent of her power—from the girl of that unhappy fortnight?

Different and strange so that his first glance at her would not resurrect those memories and start him to thinking those cold defeated thoughts again?

He did not know. As he met Harla's eyes he had the impression that she was expecting something more from him than a partnerly handshake, after their long separation. But of that too he was not mortally sure.

With his thoughts still all in a fog, he went back with her to the kitchen, where everybody seemed to have congregated; and shook hands with Strap and said hello to the Spencers. As he took a cup of tea from Eleanor, he remembered the evening three months ago when he had come here to see Herm, before pitching off on the trail of those shadows. Then he had been alone, in disgrace, his career blasted.

Now, here were four people, staunch warm friends of his; and their friendship seemed to him a richness more precious than the success of his hunt and even the position awaiting him at Ottawa.

"What's the news of the Three Rivers, Strap?" he asked, trying to be a part of the talk and laughter.

"Not much, Noel. You drained all the news off. Can't much happen down there for a long time, after all the fireworks you staged."

He flipped his cigarette ashes on the floor, out of long habit at the Buzzard Roost. "Alice Wentworth said to give you her regards. I don't know whether I will or not. I may keep 'em myself and use 'em on my Manitou stops. Corporal Schuler, that cut-and-dried piece of red tape——Say, Noel, when he found out who you really were and all about this Flood-Rocco business, he bought a gallon of whisky and went on his first toot in twenty-five years, and he's never been the same person since. Inspector Clevenger told me that if it happens again, he'll raise Schuler to a duty sergeant. Constable Brannigan, your old side-kick and pal, is at Fort James. Clevenger yanked him back there and made him official dog-feeder to the Police teams."

Noel smiled at that. Strap rambled on:

"Tah-Gomaugh wants you to come back down north, Noel, and spend a while in the Dinokui basin, inviting your soul.

Here"—he fished in his pocket and handed Noel a little scroll of birch paper—"that's his invitation. He couldn't write one, so he drew it."

Noel unrolled the odd papyrus. The invitation was in form of a small picture; a lazy sunlit river, an anchored birchbark and a man asleep in the canoe, with a trout line tied around his big toe.

"Now that," Strap said, "is a Smoky's idea of perfect bliss. Paradise. The loaf of bread, jug of wine and thou."

"It's not such a bad idea, at that," Noel commented. In his mind's eye he was seeing that lush beautiful basin and the blue-hazy peace of those dim mountains. "I hope to take Tah-Gomaugh up sometime. But just now"—he pulled his trouser pocket inside out—"what would I use for money?"

Strap blinked his eyes.

"Money? Hell's b—— I mean, my goodness, I thought you'd be hog-plastered with money! A six-seven million dollar placer——"

"That was Indian Bureau property. It was turned over to them, where it belongs."

"But didn't you get a slice or a divvy or some gravy or something?"

"I didn't ask for any, and none was offered. By and large, there's mighty little of this 'gravy' business in official Ottawa, Strap."

"Then how about the Rocco reward? That was a nifty little fortune, and who got it if you didn't?"

"I got it. But I didn't keep it. You see, Strap, that was blood money. I killed men to get Flood, so I turned that reward over to a charity."

Strap drew a deep breath and whistled. "Twenty-five thousand dollars, and you snuff it out like a candle! You're a sad, sad case of something or other."

Herm Spencer interposed. "I hate to cut in on this good rag-chewing, but somebody's got to bring you people's luggage from the station. Strap, suppose you and I get that done, and then you can chew the rag till morning." He paused, glanced knowingly at Eleanor. "How about going along, dear, and getting a breath of air?"

Eleanor caught his meaning—that Harla and Noel might have a little time alone. "Why, yes," she said tactfully, "if it wouldn't be rude of me to run out on our guests."

Their tact was completely lost on Strap. "Rude?" he snorted. "My eye! The sooner we take off, the better they'll like it. We're just cluttering up their landscape. Why, all the way out of the North—eighteen hundred miles! and then the train drag from Edmonton here, all I heard was Noel this and Noel that. Okay, let's ankle." ...

When they were gone, Harla motioned at the living room, where a bright birch fire was burning, against the chill of the October night. Her cheeks were still flushed from Strap's incriminating remarks, and she would not meet Noel's eyes.

"Shall we go in there?" she suggested.

Noel shook his head. In his feverish mood, walls seemed intolerably confining and oppressive. He wanted the largeness of the night sky and the tang of the little norther that was bringing the migrants out of the wild lands of Keewatin and Mackenzie.

As he brought a wrap for Harla and they walked out into the small rock garden where he and Spencer, one year ago, had planned the Rocco hunt, Harla tried to steer their talk into a safe channel.

"I can't tell you how glad I was, Noel, when I heard about this new position of yours. Aren't you going to say anything at all about it?"

Noel had little thought, just then, for Ottawa and his work there. Harla's nearness, the moon spangles in her hair, and, above all, Strap's guileless disclosures, made Ottawa seem far away and unimportant.

"It's a newly created post," he explained, perfunctorily, "to coordinate the work of the Mounted and Provincials and other law enforcing agencies. With a hundred and fourteen such agencies in the Dominion, there's clash and duplication. I'm to keep that down, and be a sort of consultant to them all."

"A hundred and fourteen!" Harla breathed. "That sounds like work for you, Noel!"

He nodded. Yes, it would be a hard and exacting position, but a challenging one too. It would be a work of nation-wide importance, such as he had always wanted. No more trailing individual criminals or drifting all over a continent in a nameless friendless existence. He would be living at Ottawa, living like other people, with friends and associations.

After those thirteen uprooted years, it would be like walking out of a prison into the sunshine.

As they stopped in a shaft of light from a window, he ventured, hesitantly:

"Since Manitou, since I left you there, Harla, it's seemed a long time."

She plucked at a withered rose bloom. "Has it? I didn't notice. I was so busy—working frantically; and even so I didn't get that job completed. I hope to go back next summer and finish it."

"Perhaps I can arrange a leave by then, and we could—you and I—could go together."

"It would be an awf'ly nice trip," she admitted. "But for us to pitch off like that, so far away from everybody—wouldn't it be just a little bit scandalous, Noel?"

"Harla! Please. You know what I'm meaning—how I'd want us to go. And you know why it's been so long for me since Manitou." He took her hands in his and kept her from turning away from him. "Ever since I met you at McMurray, *you've* known."

"But you, Noel, there at Manitou—you wrote me off——"

"I tried to. But I couldn't. Harla—?"

She knew what he wanted to do—and yet was so awkward and hesitant and inept at doing—as he stood there with her hands in his. From his first word and glance that evening, she had known what was in his heart toward her; and that knowledge had brought her a singing happiness.

"Harla—?" he repeated.

She looked up at him then. "Yes?"

"May I, dear?"

The very artlessness of the question made Harla smile. But the smile died on her lips. Back of his artlessness toward her, back of his whole ineptness and hesitancy, lay his lonely years, his long shadow years; and she could not smile at those. The tears sprang to her eyes at the mere thought of them. As her fingers tightened upon his and she stood tiptoe, she whispered:

"I've been wanting you to, Noel."

THE END

www.ingramcontent.com/pod-product-compliance
Lightning Source LLC
Chambersburg PA
CBHW031231260626
47169CB00007B/2246